A TIME TO ABIDE

A CHRISTIAN ROMANCE

JULIETTE DUNCAN

A TIME FOR EVERYTHING SERIES - BOOK 3

PRAISE FOR "A TIME TO ABIDE"

"WOW! How does Juliette continue to improve her stories each time. This story is so full of the full range of emotions. Joy to heartache to fear and trust. An easy story to read of how God works through the frailty of His children to bring hope to those who need it."
~Margaret L

"This book is truly amazing inspirational story that you won't be able to stop reading. Bruce and Wendy are very special people...I would give this book a higher rating than a five star review if I could." *~ Debbie*

"Rarely do I give a 5 star review, but this book certainly warrants a top rating. Juliette weaves a beautiful story of forgiveness and trust. This book brough tears to my eyes several times. I love how she uses her characters to show us how to trust God in struggles we all face in our own lives." *~Jan*

"Juliette Duncan has once again written a story that encompasses all your emotions like a ride on a run away roller coaster." *~Jana*

FOREWORD

HELLO! Thank you for choosing to read this book - I hope you enjoy it! Please note that this story is told from two different points of view – Wendy, an Australian, and Bruce, a cowboy from Texas. Australian spelling and terminology have been used when in Wendy's point of view – they're not typos!

As a thank you for reading this book, I'd like to offer you a FREE GIFT. That's right - my FREE novella, "Hank and Sarah - A Love Story" is available exclusively to my newsletter subscribers. Go to http://www.julietteduncan.com/subscribe to get the ebook for FREE, and to be notified of future releases.

I hope you enjoy both books! Have a wonderful day!

Juliette

PROLOGUE

"There is a time for everything,
and a season for every activity under the heavens:
a time to be born and a time to die,
a time to plant and a time to uproot,
a time to kill and a time to heal,
a time to tear down and a time to build,
a time to weep and a time to laugh,
a time to mourn and a time to dance,
a time to scatter stones and a time to gather them,
a time to embrace and a time to refrain from embracing,
a time to search and a time to give up,
a time to keep and a time to throw away,
a time to tear and a time to mend,
a time to be silent and a time to speak,
a time to love and a time to hate,
a time for war and a time for peace."
Ecclesiastes 3:1-8

CHAPTER 1

S ydney, Australia

DURING THE WEEKS following the death of Paige, Wendy McCarthy's much-loved adult daughter, the birth of her granddaughter, and the discovery that her son, Simon, was gay, Wendy sought solace in her Bible. She knew that a faith relationship with God didn't shield her from heartache, but grief had closed in on her heart like a murky blanket of fog and she was suffocating under its weight.

She'd been there before. When Greg, her first husband, died suddenly of a heart attack six years earlier, she'd walked the valley of grief for many months. Even now, grief over losing him had never truly left her. She'd not gotten over it as some well-meaning people had told her she would. Instead, she'd learned to live with it. It had become part of her, and even when she and Bruce married and she experienced the joy of second love, her heart still grew heavy whenever memories of Greg surfaced. He'd been her first love, the father of her children. The man she'd given her heart and life to. He would always hold a special place in her heart, even now that she and Bruce were happily married.

Paige's death had also been unexpected. At thirty-four weeks pregnant she'd suffered extreme and sudden preeclampsia and had died giving birth. Baby Elysha had been the blessing that helped Wendy through her initial grief, but Paige was gone, and a hole remained in Wendy's heart. She blamed herself. If she hadn't left her phone at home that afternoon, Paige might have received treatment sooner and could still be alive. Bruce had told her she couldn't take the blame. Everything possible had been done to save Paige. Blaming herself wouldn't bring her back. Wendy knew that, but guilt still weighed heavily on her and dragged her down.

Wendy's Texan husband had been a tower of strength since Paige's death. She couldn't have survived without him. Bruce often found her sitting on Paige's bed in tears. He'd sit beside her and hold her as she wept. He, too, had walked the valley of grief after his first wife died in a car accident, and he knew how she felt. He knew the utter despair that gripped her at times and sent her spiralling towards depression. He knew the ever-present heaviness that sat in her stomach like a lead weight. She thanked God every day that he was in her life.

The week between Paige's death and her funeral had in many ways been easier than now. Adrenalin had kept her going then, but now, all that was left were memories and an empty house. So often she expected Paige to walk through the door, but she never did. Her beautiful daughter was gone from their lives. Wendy's only solace was that Paige had recommitted her life to the Lord the night before she died, almost as if she knew her time on earth would be cut short. They'd buried her beside Greg, the father Paige loved so much, and now Wendy imagined them reunited, looking down from above.

She sipped the tea that Bruce had set on her nightstand before he went on his early morning horse ride and continued reading Psalm 34.

Taste and see that the Lord is good; blessed is the one who takes refuge in Him. Fear the Lord, you His holy people, for those who fear Him lack nothing. The lions may grow weak and hungry, but those who seek the Lord lack no good thing. Come, my children, listen to me; I will teach you the fear of the Lord. Whoever of you loves life and desires to see many good days, keep your tongue from evil and your lips from telling lies. Turn from evil and do good; seek peace and pursue it.

The righteous cry out, and the Lord hears them; He delivers them from all their troubles. The Lord is close to the brokenhearted and saves those who are crushed in spirit. The righteous person may have many troubles, but the Lord delivers him from them all.

She closed her Bible and her eyes. "Thank You, Lord. I believe Your Word, although my spirit is crushed. Lift me, sustain me. Teach me through this time of grieving as I draw close to You. You are the great comforter, and I seek Your face. Give me strength for this day, dear Lord, that's all I ask. In Jesus' precious name. Amen."

Bruce's soft voice echoed her 'Amen'. Wendy opened her eyes and smiled. "How long have you been there, my darling?"

"Just long enough to hear your beautiful prayer." As he returned her smile, his crystal blue eyes, full of compassion and love, melted her heart. He moved closer and sat beside her. Took her hand. Drew it to his lips and kissed it. "How are you this morning, my love?"

She sighed. "I feel like sleeping all day, but I won't."

He stroked her hand. "There's no need to get up. You know that."

"I do, but I think I'd like to go to the cemetery today, and maybe to the hospital to visit Elysha."

"Whatever you want, darling. As long as you feel up to it. Would you like some breakfast?"

She shook her head. "I'm not hungry at the moment. I'll have something later." She'd completely lost her appetite and ate only because she had to.

"More tea?"

She smiled. "That would be lovely, thank you."

"My pleasure. Stay here and I'll bring it up."

She squeezed his hand. "You're too good to me."

Leaning forward, he popped a kiss on her cheek. "I'll be right back."

After he left, she closed her eyes again. She felt so terrible. Bruce's family had planned to come for Christmas but they cancelled not long after hearing about Paige's death, even though she'd encouraged them to come. Somehow, she would have coped. Today was the day they would have arrived. It had been eighteen months since Bruce had seen his Texan family, and she knew how much he'd been looking forward to their visit. His grandchildren wouldn't remember him if they put it off too long. Skype was great, but it wasn't the same as seeing them face to face.

She let out a long sigh. They should have come. Instead of sharing Christmas with his family, she and Bruce would now be sharing it with Simon, his partner Andy, and possibly Natalie and Adam, depending on what happened with baby Elysha. Natalie, Wendy's eldest daughter, and her husband, Adam, were officially adopting the little girl. Having undergone two unsuccessful IVF attempts, it was unlikely they would have children of their own, and Paige, with no partner or husband, had already offered Elysha to them before she had second thoughts and decided to keep her.

Elysha was a special blessing for them all and Wendy had no doubt Natalie and Adam would be wonderful parents. They all hoped that Elysha might be home for Christmas, but although she was doing well, it was highly unlikely. Born prematurely, she'd only just started gaining weight and was still having trouble feeding. Natalie and Adam spent almost all their time at the hospital. The timing was perfect because they were teachers and school was closed for the summer.

The revelation of Simon's sexuality on the night of Paige's death had shocked Wendy. She'd missed the signs entirely, although in hindsight she realised they'd been evident for a long time. Simon's secrecy over his private life, the fact that he hadn't had a girlfriend for many years, and his close friendship with his housemate, Andy, a handsome, easy-going young man she'd warmed to immediately. *Before she knew he was her son's partner.* If she'd discovered the truth at any other time, she may have reacted differently. She still didn't know how she should respond as a Christian parent, but having just lost one child, she didn't want to lose another, and so she'd refrained from saying anything that might have made him defensive.

She felt uncomfortable knowing Simon and Andy were in a relationship. No one else they knew had gay children, and coming from a conservative church background, the teaching she'd received was that homosexuality was a sin. That didn't help in working out what her response should be to her only son. There'd be time to explore that further, once she'd gotten through this intense time of grieving, but for now, she'd decided to love him, regardless. Maybe losing one child had made her appreciate the other two more. And surely Jesus would have loved Simon, the person, even if He didn't love the sin.

Bruce knocked quietly and reappeared with her tea, placing it on her nightstand. "There you are, darlin'. Let me know if you'd like anything else."

"Thank you. This is lovely." She smiled at him and lifted the cup to her lips. She took a sip and set it down. "How was your ride this morning?"

"Peaceful. You should come with me one morning."

Wendy let out a small whimper. She'd only ridden once since they'd moved to their ten-acre hobby farm in the Hills District of Sydney. The day that Paige had her attack. The day she left her phone at home. As much as she knew Bruce would love her to go with him, she couldn't relive that particular memory yet. Maybe in time, but not yet. "One day, darling. Not yet."

"I know. We can always take a walk instead."

"I'd like that."

"Let me know when you're ready."

Wendy smiled. She appreciated Bruce's understanding so much. He wasn't pushing her to do things, but instead, he was giving her time to grieve and to take things slowly. They both knew that grief couldn't be rushed. "Maybe tomorrow morning, but let me see how I'm feeling."

"No problem. What time did you want to leave this morning?"

"As soon as I'm ready, if that's okay with you."

"That's fine. I'll get cleaned up and be ready whenever you are."

She squeezed his hand and gazed into his eyes. "I love you, Bruce."

"And I love you, Wendy. You're a special woman, and I feel honoured to be on this journey with you."

"And I feel blessed that you are." She drew him to her side. He slid his arm around her and hugged her tight. In his arms, her sadness lifted a little.

CHAPTER 2

*W*endy sat quietly with her hands folded in her lap and stared out the window at the passing scenery. It hardly seemed any time at all since they'd first driven out to the Hills District to look at properties, and yet, so much had changed. She sometimes missed her old home on the harbour, though she was happy they'd moved. Bruce had his horses and open spaces, and she was learning to love the area renowned for its trendy cafés, boutique shops and art galleries. And they were making their own memories. Although there was one memory she wished they didn't have.

Bruce slowed the car when they approached the village. "Would you like to stop for coffee?" They were passing the 'Wheel and Barrow', the café they'd brunched at the first morning they'd visited the area.

Although tempting, Wendy shook her head. Everyone in the tight-knit community knew about Paige, and whenever she met anyone, they offered condolences and well-meaning platitudes. While she appreciated their compassion and concern, right now, she didn't want to see anyone other than family. That would pass in time, but right now her grief was raw and she ended up in tears at the first kind word from a well-meaning acquaintance or stranger. But she did need to get some flowers. "Can we stop at the flower stall?"

Bruce smiled. "Sure."

Approaching the roadside flower stall on the edge of town, Bruce slowed the car and stopped on the verge. A rotund Islander woman wearing a colourful dress printed with large hibiscus flowers sat on a folding chair under a large beach umbrella, fanning herself. Two small children with dark, curly hair played on the grass at her feet. The woman, Rosy Fifita, eased herself out of the chair and waved.

Bruce turned to Wendy. "Would you like me to go?"

Wendy sighed. Rosy was a friendly woman and might be offended if she stayed in the car. "No, I can do it."

The corners of Bruce's eyes crinkled when he smiled and squeezed her hand. He knew how difficult this was for her, and she appreciated his support.

Opening the door, Wendy planted a smile on her face and walked towards Rosy. "How are you today, Rosy? The flowers look beautiful."

"Oh, I'm wonderful, thank you. But 'ow are you? I was so sad to hear 'bout yer daughta. Are you gettin' flowers for 'er?"

"Yes, I am. And I'm doing well, thanks."

"That's good to 'ear. What would you like? I've got some lovely mixed bunches."

"That will be fine. I'll take one of them, thank you."

Rosy pulled a big, colourful bunch from her bucket, placed

it inside a plastic cover, and handed it to Wendy.

Wendy smiled and took the bunch. "Thank you, Rosy. They're lovely." She pulled out her purse. "How much?"

"My gift. For 'yer daughta."

Tears welled within Wendy's eyes. "Thank you. That's so kind."

"You're welcome. I know what it's like to lose a young 'un. It's a sad time for sure."

"It is." Wendy swallowed the lump in her throat. "You have a wonderful day, Rosy. You and your beautiful children." She smiled at the two tiny tots who were still playing happily together.

"Thank you. God bless."

"And you." Wendy smiled and then walked back to the car. Talking about Paige's death was so hard, but she needed to accept with gratitude the kindness of others. Death brought people together. Made them more compassionate, caring, understanding. Lowering her nose to the beautiful bunch of flowers, she inhaled the sweet perfume and was reminded of the proverb, *Oil and perfume make the heart glad, so a man's counsel is sweet to his friend.*

Sliding onto the seat beside Bruce, Wendy took a moment to gather her composure, finally lifting her gaze. "She's a kind lady."

The warmth of his smile echoed in his voice. "And so are you." His gaze connected with hers and fresh tears sprang to her eyes. She sucked in a big breath. "Let's keep going. I don't want these flowers to wilt, nor do I want to end up in tears." He squeezed her shoulder and started the car.

She settled into her seat and closed her eyes.

The cemetery, almost an hour's drive away, was near Wendy's previous home on the harbour. They'd chosen to bury Paige there so her body would be next to her father's. Not that it mattered. Only their decaying bodies remained, but visiting their graves gave Wendy a focus, and for now, it helped.

Almost an hour later, Bruce gently shook her. "We've arrived, darlin'."

Wendy blinked and straightened. Positioned on a hill overlooking the Pacific Ocean, the cemetery had a wonderful vista, with the sparkling ocean stretching as far as the eye could see. Often the wind howled a gale and it was difficult to walk upright, but today, as Wendy stepped out of the car, a gentle breeze greeted her, and the sun warmed her face as if God knew He needed to treat her kindly.

Bruce took her hand. "Are you okay?"

She nodded. "Yes."

Greg and Paige were buried in Row 567. Reaching the row, they turned left. Greg's grave was the third on the right, Paige's the fourth. Wendy's gaze paused briefly on Greg's grave and headstone. She knew the epitaph by heart. She blinked back tears. Bruce squeezed her hand. Her gaze shifted to the fresh gravesite beside it. They'd erected a temporary headstone, a timber cross with the verse they'd chosen together blazed into it.

I sought the Lord and He heard me
and delivered me from all my fears. Psalm 34:4

Wendy bent down and touched the cross. She knew that Paige was in a better place. Her troubled life on earth was over,

13

and she *was* delivered of all her fears, but it didn't seem real. How could her beautiful vibrant daughter be dead? A shudder raced through Wendy's body and deep, gutteral sobs overtook her. Falling to her knees, she wept. For a long moment, time stood still. Memories of Paige flashed through her mind, and with each memory, fresh sobs erupted.

Finally, a gentle hand on her shoulder calmed her. *Bruce.* She opened her eyes and looked up. Lifting her arms, she allowed him to help her stand. He held her tight as she sobbed into his shoulder. Her heart ached like it had never ached before. Such intense grief she'd never known.

"It's okay, Wendy. Let it out." He stroked her hair and prayed quietly. "Lord God, bless my dear Wendy. Comfort her in her grief. Uphold her in her lament. Make Your face shine upon her and give her peace."

Her sobs slowly eased, and she pulled back and wiped her eyes. "Thank you, darling. I'm sorry."

"You've got nothing to be sorry about."

She sniffed. Blew her nose. "I know, but thank you anyway."

He pulled her close again and kissed the side of her head. Above, seagulls squawked and a slight breeze started up, ruffling her hair gently. The smell of the ocean filled her nostrils. She inhaled it deeply. Fresh, clean, salty air. Slowly, she grew calm and peace filled her heart. She would survive this. The pain would lessen, but she'd never forget her beautiful daughter.

Placing the flowers at the foot of the cross, she lifted her palm to her lips and then touched it to the grave. "God bless you, Paige. I love you."

She and Bruce arrived at the hospital half an hour later.

After parking the car, Bruce took Wendy's hand and together they walked to the lift. He pressed the button for level eight—the neonatal ward. Photos of tiny babies and their mothers filled the wall of the walkway. Before and after photos. The walkway would never display a 'before' photo. Paige didn't get to see Elysha. Never got to hold her. Wendy had to stop thinking like that because it only caused more grief. She needed to focus on the 'after' photo. Little Elysha had a mother, a mother who loved her dearly. She might not be her natural mother, but Natalie loved her as if she were.

When they reached the ward, Natalie was sitting in a chair feeding her tiny baby. She looked up and grinned. "Hello, Mum."

"Hello, sweetheart." Stepping closer, she kissed Natalie's cheek then bent down and smiled at her granddaughter. "How is she doing?"

Natalie beamed. "Great. She's put on a hundred grams since the weekend."

"That's wonderful. She's so precious." Wendy fought to control her emotions.

"She is. Would you like to finish feeding her?"

"I'd love to. As long as it's all right."

Natalie smiled. "It is. Take a seat and I'll pass her to you."

Wendy settled herself into a chair beside Natalie. She'd only held Elysha once, on the day of Paige's funeral, when her emotions were raw and her heart breaking. Today, although she was still grieving, she felt more at peace as she cocooned Elysha in her arms.

She was so thin, but she was gaining weight every day. Maybe not enough to be home for Christmas, but possibly soon after. Wendy settled her and took the bottle from Natalie. The last time she'd done this was when Paige was a baby, but she wouldn't let her thoughts drift. Elysha deserved her to be in the present. To be fully there, in the here and now, not in the past. She smiled as the baby began sucking. Wrapped in a soft blanket, Elysha looked content and happy. Maybe it was because she knew how much she was loved.

Gazing at Bruce and Natalie, Wendy could barely contain her joy. Maybe God was using this tiny girl to heal their broken hearts.

THEY STAYED at the hospital for the next two hours. It was a joy and a comfort to watch Elysha sleep, to see the way Natalie beamed when she held her, to see the love in her eyes. When Adam arrived for lunch, it warmed Wendy's heart to witness the love he showered upon both Natalie and Elysha. This wasn't how they'd planned to become parents, but it truly didn't matter. They were a family, and God had blessed them in the most unexpected way.

Wendy was reluctant to leave. Being here with Elysha gave her a sense of peace, but Natalie and Adam needed time together, with Elysha. She gave Elysha another kiss and then turned to Natalie. "Take care, sweetheart. We'd love you to come for Christmas lunch, but we'll understand if you can't make it."

"We're planning on coming, with or without Elysha," Natalie replied.

"That's wonderful. We'll look forward to seeing you." Wendy hugged her and Adam, and then she and Bruce left.

Bruce placed his arm on her shoulder as they headed to the lift. "They're a lovely family."

Wendy agreed. They were. God had truly blessed them. But the mention of Christmas had sent her mind whirling, and on the way home in the car she sat quietly while staring out the window. How would she cope eating turkey opposite her son and his gay partner? Chatting and laughing as if their relationship was normal? The thought tore at her insides. Made her ill. *How had Simon become gay?*

Ten minutes into the trip, Bruce took her hand. "Are you okay, darlin'? You're awfully quiet."

She shrugged. "Yes and no."

"Want to talk?"

She drew a deep breath and faced him. "I don't know that I can do Christmas lunch with Simon and Andy. I know I should be able to, but I truly don't know that I can. Every time I think about them being a couple, I feel sick."

"Oh, Wendy. My darlin'. Somehow, we've got to. I don't know how to handle it either, but I think that we just have to treat them as if they were like any other couple."

"I don't think I can. I'm afraid I'll say something that will upset Simon, and then that will be that. We'll have lost him. It might be better for them not to come at all." She held back a sob.

Bruce squeezed her hand across the seat. "We can do this, Wendy. If we tell ourselves that they're best friends and try not to think about anything else, it should be okay."

"But what if they hold hands? *Or kiss?*" She bit her lip and breathed slowly.

"We'll ask them not to."

17

"Simon won't like that. He's never liked being told what to do."

"I can have a word with him."

"He'll like that even less."

"We'll just have to trust their judgment, then. Simon must know that you wouldn't feel comfortable with them showing affection. I'm sure he understands that you're still adjusting to the situation and learning to accept it."

She nodded. "I assume that's why he kept his secret from me for so long."

"I'm sure it will be okay. We might just need to get used to them being a couple."

Wendy cringed. "I don't want to get used to it. Why can't he be normal?" She knew she sounded petulant, but she truly didn't know if she could accept her son being gay.

Bruce replied calmly. "If this is how he's chosen to live, we might have to accept it."

A shudder raced up her spine. "I need to talk to him."

"Wait until after Christmas?" Bruce lifted a brow.

She let out an exasperated sigh. "I guess so. I'll do my best to keep a handle on my emotions until then." She felt and sounded defeated. She could hear it in her own voice. But how could they celebrate the birth of Jesus while her son was so obviously going against what He intended for his life? Maybe she was being too negative. She'd had little exposure to homo-sexuals and it was all new to her. Maybe she was being old-fashioned. But it didn't sit right. However, like Bruce said, maybe they *would* need to get used to it. Either that or lose her son. Bitter tears welled in her eyes as she turned her head and stared out the window. *God, You've got to help us.*

CHAPTER 3

The following morning, while Wendy was baking some Christmas treats, the phone rang. It was Natalie, and she was in tears. Wendy could barely make out what she was saying. She turned down the volume of the music she had playing in the background so she could hear her better. "Slow down, sweetheart. What's the matter?" Although she tried to remain clam, Wendy's heart pounded. *Had something happened to Elysha?*

Natalie sniffed. "I'm sorry. It was such a shock."

"What was?" Wendy's mind whirled. What was going on?

Natalie blew her nose before replying. "Elysha's father turned up at the hospital." The words tumbled out of her mouth.

Wendy frowned. "Paige never said who the father was. I didn't think she knew."

"It seems that one of her Goth friends worked out who it was and told him. It's Colin. Colin Daley."

A small breath blew from Wendy's mouth. She'd never met the man, but he'd hurt Paige badly when he ended their relationship earlier in the year. "What does he want?"

"I don't know yet. The hospital staff are talking with him. They want to be sure that he is the father, and then, I guess we might have to fight for custody if he decides he wants Elysha." Natalie burst into tears again.

How Wendy wished she was there to hold her daughter. After all they'd been through, this wasn't fair. "Stay calm, Natalie. I'll come to the hospital. Is Adam with you?"

"Yes, he is. There's no need to come in, Mum. Just pray."

"I can do that, but are you sure? I can be there in half an hour."

"Yes. I'll let you know if anything changes."

"Okay, sweetheart. I'll be praying." After she ended the call, Wendy cast her gaze over the kitchen counter covered in trays, bowls, sugar and flour. She'd only been baking as a way of attempting to get into the Christmas spirit. Now her heart wasn't in it at all. What did sweet treats matter when a baby's future was at stake?

She gathered everything together and threw a cloth over it all. Maybe she'd finish baking later, maybe not. Her heart was heavy as she went outside to find Bruce. Since they'd moved to the farm, he was always tinkering with something or other if he wasn't riding. Today he was working on an old tractor that had seen better days. Wendy didn't know what they needed a tractor for, but he assured her it would come in handy.

Reaching the large shed, she peered inside. Bruce's legs stuck out from under the tractor. He was obviously engrossed in whatever he was doing. She shouldn't disturb him. Other than pray, there was nothing he could do either. She withdrew quietly and wandered to the rose garden that had become her place of respite. The previous owners had a penchant for roses and at least twenty varieties filled the circular garden with colour and perfume. A paved path led around the garden, and a bench seat, positioned under a jacaranda tree, provided the perfect place to enjoy the display.

Sitting, Wendy drew a slow breath. How much more could they bear? Surely Colin Daley wouldn't want Elysha. *Did fathering a child make you a father?* He'd had nothing to do with Paige during her pregnancy. She must have known who the father was when her dates were confirmed, but she'd never said a word, suggesting strongly that she didn't want him involved. But maybe he had a legal right. Paige hadn't left a will. Natalie and Adam therefore had no legal right to Elysha, although until Colin Daley appeared on the scene, the adoption process had been going smoothly. They'd be devastated if they lost her now.

Just thinking of it tore at Wendy's insides. She did the only thing that would make a difference and bowed her head. "Oh, God, I call on You now. Take control of this situation and let sense prevail. Let Colin Daley see that Elysha will be better off with Natalie and Adam. They love her dearly and have already invested so much into her life. It would break their hearts to give her up now. Wrap Your arms around them, Lord, and give them peace in the midst of their turmoil. Let them trust You to work this out."

She paused and inhaled slowly. "Like David, my spirit grows faint within me; my heart within me is dismayed. I remember the days of long ago; I meditate on all Your works and consider what Your hands have done. I spread out my hands to You; I thirst for You like a parched land. Answer me quickly, Lord; my spirit fails. Do not hide your face from me or I will be like those who go down to the pit. I need You, Lord, lift me up. Give me hope and peace. In Jesus' precious name. Amen."

As she tried to squelch the anguish in her heart, Wendy knew she should trust God in this situation, just like she should trust Him to work out her relationship with Simon, but her mind was languid, and a wretchedness she'd not known came over her. Hot tears rolled down her cheeks. She swiped at them and squeezed her eyes shut. Suddenly overwhelmed by the events of the past few weeks, she yielded to compulsive sobs that physically shook her body.

Do not fear, for I have redeemed you; I have called you by name, you are mine. When you pass through the waters, I will be with you; and through the rivers, they shall not overwhelm you; when you walk through fire you shall not be burned, and the flame shall not consume you. For I am the Lord your God, the Holy One of Israel, your Savior.

Little by little, her spirits lifted. God would uphold and carry her when she couldn't go on. When her heart ached and the swell of pain was beyond tears. She would get through this. And so would Natalie and Adam. They might have to fight for Elysha, but Wendy believed she would be theirs in the end. Despite this, her heart went out to Colin. What would it be like to know you had a daughter but not have anything to do with her? Wendy didn't know him, and it was wrong to judge him. But it would be complicated if he wanted to be involved in her life. More so if he contested custody.

Nothing would happen quickly, of that she was certain. Christmas Day was the following day, and all the courts and agencies would be closed for the festive period. The hospital staff would need to be on alert in case he made trouble. Natalie and Adam would be reluctant to leave Elysha's side. She wouldn't blame them. If he decided to take her, Wendy hated to think what would happen to her.

That meant that only Simon and Andy might grace their table for Christmas lunch. Wendy's stomach churned with anxiety. This Christmas should have been a wonderful time of celebration with both families coming together. Instead, Bruce's family was in Texas, Paige was dead, and Natalie and Adam would most likely spend the day at the hospital. And she and Bruce would have no excuse. They would have to face Simon and Andy and get through the day without a scene. There was no way she could do that in her own strength, so she called on God's.

CHAPTER 4

*S*imon sighed heavily as he stood in front of the mirror on Christmas morning, shaving. There had to be some way of excusing himself and Andy from lunch with Mum and Bruce. Just the previous evening she'd telephoned and told him that Natalie and Adam would no longer be coming because Colin Daley was on the scene claiming to be Elysha's father and they were concerned he might cause trouble.

He'd met the dude when Colin and Paige were a couple. He wasn't someone his mum, Natalie or Adam would want involved in Elysha's upbringing. Colin Daley was bad news. *How had Paige gotten mixed up with a dude like that?* One thing he knew for sure—Colin Daley would never be welcome in their conservative Christian family.

Simon sighed again as he squirted shaving foam onto his hand and then applied it to his face. Just like his relationship with Andy would never be accepted. He'd never forget the look on Mum's face the night Paige died. The night Mum discovered he was gay. He hadn't meant it to happen like it had. Reaching out and taking Andy's hand had been an automatic response to the news of his sister's death, and Mum noticed. He wasn't sure how she hadn't noticed before, but it confirmed to him that she'd had no suspicion whatsoever. When she realised the truth of his and Andy's relationship, it had come as a complete and utter shock.

He was waiting for her tirade. Since Paige's death she'd said nothing, but if it were just him and Andy having Christmas lunch with her and Bruce, the topic could no longer be avoided. He didn't want to discuss it with her. She was disappointed, no doubt. She might even disown him, since being gay was considered a sin in the church he'd been raised in. He knew the bigotry that existed there. He'd even felt it at Paige's funeral service. The looks. The frowns. The whispers. Word had gotten out. *Simon's gay...*

But something had shifted inside him during the service that made him start questioning who he really was. Not that he'd said anything to Andy. Or to Mum. Or to anyone. He loved Andy and couldn't imagine not being with him. But since then, he'd felt unsettled. Like God was tapping him on the shoulder. He didn't want to be tapped. He was perfectly fine the way he was. *But was he?* Paige's death had been sudden. Unexpected. Mum said she'd made peace with God the night before she died, and although Mum was grief-stricken, she knew exactly where Paige was. With Dad. With God.

If he died unexpectedly, Simon knew exactly where he'd end up. Not with Dad, and definitely not with God. He'd walked away from the faith of his childhood and chosen a lifestyle that was at odds with it. One he knew wouldn't get him into heaven. Not that he cared. Heaven was likely a myth and only existed in the minds of the hopeful. But he couldn't deny the way his heart had quickened at Paige's funeral when the pastor read from the Bible about death being swallowed up in victory for those who loved the Lord. It could have just been the emotion of the day. His sister was about to be buried beside their father. But Simon couldn't shake the feeling it was more than that. He'd keep it to himself. Andy wouldn't understand. Although he worked as a Palliative Care Nurse and witnessed death every day, Andy had no faith. His mantra was that if there was a God, life wouldn't end like it did. He'd resolved to make his patients' last days as comfortable as possible, but he could offer them no hope of anything after they took their final breath.

But what if there was something? A word he'd hate Mum to hear shot out of his mouth when he nicked his face with the razor. Quickly grabbing a tissue, he shoved it onto the cut and stemmed the flow of blood. He should stop thinking like this. It was distracting. He was happy with his life. And that's exactly what he'd tell Mum at lunch since there was no way of getting out of going. He wouldn't allow her to judge him or to cast her outdated Christian views onto him.

WENDY CLUTCHED Bruce's hand as they walked into the chapel of the Hills Christian Church on Christmas morning. She hadn't wanted to go, but Bruce had said that church was exactly the place she needed to be. He was right, of course.

Staying at home and getting wound up about lunch with Simon and Andy was no way to celebrate Christ's birthday.

Although new to the church, because of Paige's sudden passing, a lot of the faces were already familiar. Wendy nodded and smiled at Barbara, an older woman with silvery-grey short hair who'd kindly cooked several meals for them, and held her tears rigidly in check when Emily Hodges, the pastor's wife, gave her a big hug and said she was praying for her. Finally, Wendy eased herself into a pew beside Bruce. The introduction to *O Holy Night* was being played by the worship band, and as the worship leader invited the congregation to stand and sing, Wendy's spirit began to lift.

> *O holy night the stars are brightly shining*
> *It is the night of our dear Savior's birth*
> *Long lay the world in sin and error pining*
> *Till He appeared and the soul felt its worth*
> *A thrill of hope the weary world rejoices*
> *For yonder breaks a new and glorious morn*
> *Fall on your knees*
> *O hear the angels' voices*
> *O night divine*
> *O night when Christ was born*
> *O night divine o night*
> *O night divine*

Christ came to relieve the world of sin and weariness. To offer new life and the hope of a better future. That thrill of hope crept through Wendy's soul, lifting her spirit, so that all she could do was worship her Creator, and trust Him with their future.

Leaving the service a short time later, she spoke with several of the women who had also provided meals after Paige's passing. They were all so kind, and in time she felt they could become close friends. But right now, she needed to go home and finish preparations for their lunch.

"I'm so glad we went." Wendy smiled at Bruce as she fastened her seat belt. "Thanks for not letting me get my way."

He chuckled. "You're welcome. It was a lovely service."

"It was. It would have been nice if the family had shared it with us. Maybe next year."

"Yes." He reached out and squeezed her hand. "We'll get through this, Wendy. We have to trust God and allow Him to work it out."

"I know. At least Colin isn't at the hospital this morning." She'd called Natalie earlier that morning to wish her and Adam a merry Christmas. Natalie had told her that Colin had left the hospital late the previous evening. Nothing had been resolved as yet—Colin had requested a DNA test but didn't have the money to pay for it. He said he'd be back once he did. Natalie hoped that his lack of finances would help sway the adoption application their way. "And Elysha's doing well. It's a pity she isn't home for Christmas," Wendy mused.

"She'll be with us next year for sure." Bruce patted her hand before starting the car and heading out of the car park.

"Yes, for sure." She settled back into the seat. What would the next twelve months hold? She had no idea, but she knew Who held the future, and she needed to trust Him, just like Bruce said.

CHAPTER 5

*W*endy glanced out the front window when a vehicle rumbled up the driveway and came to a halt in front of the garage. It was Andy's black Hilux, complete with bullbar, chunky tyres and snorkel. As he jumped down from the driver's side, she thought, not for the first time, what an attractive young man he was. But now that she knew he was her son's partner, she looked at him with different eyes. It might be wrong, but she couldn't help it.

When he placed his arm across Simon's shoulder as the two headed for the door, she cringed and prayed once again for strength and wisdom. Drawing a steadying breath, she stopped in front of the mirror and smoothed her hair. The last few weeks had taken their toll on her appearance. Dark circles hung under her eyes despite her efforts to camouflage them. She looked tired. She felt tired.

But those who wait on the Lord shall renew their strength; They shall mount up with wings like eagles, They shall run and not be weary, They shall walk and not faint.

Thank You, Lord. Renew my strength as I wait on You.

"Darlin', they're here." Bruce's voice sounded softly behind her.

She turned around and smiled, thanking God that Bruce was here with her and she didn't have to face them alone. "Coming."

She slipped her hand into his and together they walked to the front door and greeted their guests.

Simon stepped forward and gave her a hug. "Merry Christmas, Mum." He handed her a neatly wrapped gift. Andy then hugged her and also gave her a gift. The three men shook hands. It was all a bit awkward.

"Come in. Can I get you a soft drink?" Bruce waved them inside.

"We brought beer." Simon winked, tapping the cool bag slung over his shoulder.

"Sorry. We should have bought some," Bruce replied apologetically.

"No problem. We know you don't drink alcohol."

"Let me put them in the fridge." Bruce held out his hand.

"Thanks. I'll grab two first." Simon reached into the bag and took out two beers, handing one to Andy before passing the bag to Bruce.

As Bruce headed to the kitchen, Wendy ushered Simon and Andy into the living room. Although she and Bruce had little motivation for decorations, they'd put up their Christmas tree which sat in the corner of the room. She directed the two men to the couch beside the tree and she sat opposite. Bruce returned with a plate of the Christmas treats she'd finished baking last night, a jug of punch and four glasses. He set the tray on the coffee table and offered the treats around before pouring two glasses of punch and handing her one.

She was glad of the Christmas music playing through the stereo system. It helped cover the awkwardness.

"A pity Natalie and Adam couldn't make it," Simon said after downing a rum ball.

"Yes. We might go to the hospital later and see them. It'll be a long day for them," Wendy replied.

"We might come with you."

She smiled politely, not knowing what else to do. "That would be nice."

A few moments of silence followed.

Simon took a swig of beer. "I know this is difficult for you. We don't need to stay if you don't want us here."

Wendy closed her eyes momentarily. Had she already made them feel unwelcome? She blew out a breath and opened her eyes. Bruce squeezed her hand. He was letting her respond. In many ways, she wished he'd taken the lead, but this was between her and Simon. "I'm sorry, Simon. You're right. It *is* difficult, but we *do* want you here. I think it'll be better if we talk about it. Clear the air."

"If that's what you want."

"It is." Wendy unclenched the fist she hadn't realised she'd been clenching.

Bruce nodded to Andy. Without a word, they stood and walked outside, leaving her and Simon alone.

Wendy slowly lifted her gaze to her son. It grieved her that she no longer knew him. He'd shut her out of his life, and now she knew why. "I...I don't know what to say, Simon. Finding out you're gay caught me by surprise. I had no idea."

"I didn't know how to tell you."

"How...how long?"

"Three years."

"Three years?" She ran her hand over her hair. "I feel so stupid."

"Don't. You had no way of knowing."

"I guess not, but still, I should have sensed something."

"So, what do you think? I guess you don't approve."

"I'm...I'm not comfortable with your choice of lifestyle. But you know that already."

"Yes."

"What I don't understand is why? Why did you choose to be gay?" She pleaded with him, desperately wanting to know.

"I didn't choose it, Mum. It's the way I am."

Their gazes locked. "I don't understand. You've had girlfriends."

"They never lasted. It never felt right."

"Maybe you just didn't meet the right girl."

He shrugged. "I love Andy."

She was lost for words. "I don't know how to handle that."

He took another sip of his beer and leaned forward, crossing his legs. "You either accept it or you don't. Andy's family is fine with our relationship." He held her gaze, throwing out a challenge.

"I don't know that I can ever be fine with you living a gay life, Simon. You know it goes against what I believe."

"But times have changed. Maybe you need to move on from your outdated beliefs."

"But some things are black and white. I think this is one of them, but I can't tell you how to live your life. If you choose to live this way, then that's your decision, but I don't think I can ever be fine with it."

"We should leave. I knew it was a bad decision to come."

She reached out to him. "Don't do that. I'm sorry. We have to work this out somehow. I've already lost Paige. I don't want to lose you as well."

His lips twitched. She knew he missed her, too. It was a grief they shared. "How are you doing, Mum?"

She shrugged. "Some days are better than others."

"I know. I still can't believe she's gone."

"I still expect her to walk through the door."

"I'm sorry I've disappointed you." He lifted his gaze and met hers again.

Tears stung her eyes. Quickly moving to the couch, she sat beside him and slipped her arms around him. "I love you, Simon." Her voice choked. "I'm sorry for not approving of your lifestyle, but let's work through it."

He nodded. "Andy's talking about getting married."

Wendy blinked. If he'd made the comment for shock value, it worked. "Married?" She pulled back and stared at him.

He nodded again.

"How do you feel about that?"

"I'm not sure."

Relief filled her. At least there was hope. "Think about it carefully. Being gay is one thing, but getting married is another."

"I know. I'd be damned forever."

She shook her head. "No one's damned forever if they repent."

"I don't think I believe all of that anymore."

"Are you sure?" Something in his manner suggested that what his words and tone didn't exactly reflect what he thought.

"The church has a lot to answer for. The way they treat gays, for one."

"That's true. The church does have a lot to answer for, but that doesn't negate the fundamental truths of the gospel message. That God sent His perfect Son to earth as a human to save mankind from sin and to offer all who believe a future and a hope. If it wasn't true, why do we still celebrate Jesus' birth more than two thousand years later? It would have been forgotten by now if it hadn't happened."

She sensed that he was weighing up her words. As a History lecturer for many years, she knew she had the edge on him. She'd studied the historical proof of Jesus' life and death and on several occasions had discussed it with the children. It was important for them to know that it wasn't just a made-up story. That there was historical proof for Jesus' miraculous birth and resurrection, even though the majority of people, both past and present, chose to disbelieve it or ignore it. But that didn't mean it didn't happen. "Do you want me to bring the books out?"

"No." He sounded and looked defeated. It wasn't what she'd intended.

"I'm sorry. I shouldn't have attacked you like that."

"It's okay."

"I don't know how we can manage this, but let's try to treat each other with respect, and let's keep talking about the issue. We won't get anywhere otherwise."

"As long as you don't preach to me."

"I'll try not to." She smiled. "Give me a hug?"

As he returned her smile, she noticed that his eyes had watered. She pulled him close and held him while she silently prayed for him.

After releasing him, she reached under the Christmas tree and pulled out a gift wrapped in silver paper with a matching bow on top. "Merry Christmas, Simon."

"Thank you. Have you opened yours yet?"

"No, I haven't." She'd placed the two gifts beside the couch when she first entered the room. She stood and retrieved them and sat back beside him. "It doesn't quite feel like Christmas, does it?" she asked as she began unwrapping one gift.

"No, it doesn't."

She remembered the happy Christmases before death intruded and changed their lives forever, and guessed he was remembering them too.

She smiled. "A new nightie. How lovely!" She leaned over and kissed him. "Thank you."

"You're welcome. I hope you like cotton and lace."

"It's perfect. Now, open yours."

"If it's pyjamas, I'll laugh."

"It's not pyjamas."

He ripped off the paper like a small child again and couldn't wait to see what Santa had brought him. His eyes moistened as the gift was revealed. "It's lovely. Thank you."

She smiled through her own tears. She and Bruce had deliberated over what to get him. In the end, the only thing that seemed appropriate was a framed photo of him and Paige. "I hope it doesn't make you sad."

"No. It's great. It'll help me remember her as she used to be."

"Cheeky and fun loving."

"Hot headed and annoying."

"But we loved her."

"Yes." He suddenly erupted into sobs. She pulled him close while he wept against her chest.

It hurt so much. Even though Wendy knew Paige was in a better place, she was no longer with them. They'd never see her get married or hold baby Elysha. They'd never hear her laughter again, or her terse words. They could only remember.

"I love you, Simon." She kissed the top of his head. They'd get through this bump in the road. She had no idea how, but for the first time in many years, she felt close to her son.

NATALIE'S FACE lit up when Wendy and Bruce arrived at the hospital later that afternoon. Simon and Andy had decided to go home after lunch instead of going to the hospital. They'd visit another day. Wendy guessed they had a lot to talk about. She was pleased with the way the conversation with Simon had gone, although she doubted anything would change in a hurry, if ever. As much as she hated to admit it, Simon and Andy seemed happy together. She still couldn't get her head around it. It seemed foreign. Strange. Wrong. But at least they'd all gotten through the day and they were still talking.

Elysha was asleep in Natalie's arms, a perfect picture of mother and daughter. Wendy prayed that picture would never change. "Merry Christmas!" She bent down and kissed Natalie's cheek. "How are you doing?"

"Good. The staff have been great today."

"You must be tired."

Natalie nodded. "A little."

"Would you like a break? Bruce and I can stay with Elysha if you'd like to stretch your legs."

"That would be nice. Adam's gone to get a coffee. I could go and find him."

"Why don't you do that? No need to hurry back. We'll be fine, won't we, darling?" Wendy tapped Bruce's arm.

He let out a small chuckle. "Absolutely. We know what we're doing. You can trust us." His eyes twinkled. He didn't have a clue.

"All right, then. And maybe we can have dinner together. Although I'm not sure where we'll find something decent. Christmas dinner in the hospital cafeteria would be a sad affair."

"I came prepared. I brought a picnic," Wendy said.

Natalie laughed. "Of course you did." She stood and carefully passed Elysha to her mother. "Call the nurse if you need anything. She's just had a feed so she might need to burp. I'll let the nurse know you're here on my way out. Oh, and I doubt Colin Daley will turn up, but call me straight away if he does." Her smile fell.

"I will, don't worry. And please don't hurry. We'll be fine." Wendy smiled at Natalie as she turned to leave, and then shifted her gaze to the baby who looked just like Paige when she was small. Her face was a perfect oval, her lips, exquisitely dainty. Although tiny, she was perfect in every way. "We love you, little Elysha. God bless you and keep you." She lowered her lips and placed a soft kiss on the top of the baby's downy head.

CHAPTER 6

*S*imon sat quietly on the ride home with Andy. The day had gone better than expected. He and Mum had actually spoken civilly and she hadn't grown angry and upset like he thought she would. Andy had been at ease like he always was. But Andy's family was like that. They let everyone do their own thing without judging them. His sister was a social worker who was outspoken about women's rights. She lived with her long-time partner, a male, and they had three children. They weren't married, and it seemed they were happy that way. But Andy was pressing him to get married. Simon wasn't so sure about making that kind of pledge. Like Mum said, it was a big commitment. Was he really ready to commit his life forever to another man?

He turned and studied Andy's profile. They'd met at a party three years ago, not long after Simon had ended his relationship with Sally, his girlfriend of several months. He hadn't been as dedicated to the relationship as she'd wanted him to be. Not that she wasn't a nice girl. She was. With long, blonde hair and legs that went forever, she was also smart and fun to be with, but he didn't love her. Just like he hadn't loved any of the girlfriends before her. His heart had never pounded for any of them like it did when his gaze first landed on Andy Lamond. That was the night he first realised he might be gay.

They'd spent the evening chatting. Andy was a nurse. Simon guessed he was good at his job. He had a knack of making him feel at ease, and Simon guessed he had that effect on his patients, too.

When Andy suggested they meet up again, Simon readily agreed. Before long, they were a couple. That was three years ago. Only Paige had known. It hadn't seemed to bother her that her brother was gay. Pain squeezed his heart. It wasn't fair that she was gone. Although they'd had a love-hate relationship, she was his sister, and he missed her terribly.

Andy turned and looked at him. "A penny for your thoughts."

Simon sniffed. "I was just thinking about Paige."

Andy's face softened. "Your mother's doing really well."

Simon shrugged. "I guess she is, especially since it hasn't been very long."

"It takes a long time to get over losing someone. In fact, you never really do. You just learn to live with it."

"And I guess you know that."

"Yep. I see it all the time."

Simon settled back in his seat and studied his nails. "She believes that Paige is with God. I think she might be right."

"You don't believe all that, do you? I thought you'd put that religious nonsense away."

"I'm not sure. I used to believe." He shrugged. "Maybe I still do."

Andy tapped the wheel. "Does that mean you want to break up?"

"No. Nothing like that. I'm sorry. I've just started thinking about things since Paige died. That's all."

"I think we should set a date."

Simon's head snapped up, his eyes widening. "To get married?"

Andy nodded. "I don't see any reason to wait."

Simon's heart beat faster. Could he really marry Andy? Could he ignore that little voice inside him that told him it was wrong? That same little voice that had probably stopped Paige from getting an abortion? He knew how she felt now. Their parents had instilled their Christian values into them so much when they were young that it was hard to go against them. But Andy would never understand. He bit his lip. "Sure, why not? The sooner the better."

"Great. Let's do it."

"Now?"

"No, silly. There's a lot to organise."

"We won't have a big wedding, will we?" Simon began to panic. Mum would be horrified. She wouldn't come.

"Why not? We have a lot of friends and family."

"Right." Simon gulped. "I don't think Mum will come."

"I'll sweet talk her. Wait and see."

"She does like you, even though you're gay." Simon let out a small laugh. He'd been amazed at how well Mum had warmed to Andy when they first met. And even after she knew he was gay she'd still been polite, if not a little stiff. But if anyone could talk her around, it would be Andy.

"I'm excited. I can't wait to be your husband." Smiling, he reached out his hand.

"And what does that make me?"

"*My* husband! Silly."

Two husbands. It didn't sound right. "Do...do you want children as well?" Maybe that was why Andy was so keen to get married. The thought horrified Simon.

"Maybe. But not for a while. Are you okay with that?"

Simon gulped. "I haven't thought about it."

"There's no hurry. And it'll be complicated."

It sure would be... how did two gay men go about having children? Adoption? Surrogacy? *Was that even legal?* And who would be *mum*? Simon guessed it would be him. Or would they both be dads? The more he considered it, the more it confused him. But maybe it was just his upbringing and he needed to fully let go of those outdated beliefs, like he'd told Mum to. He loved Andy. He wouldn't risk losing him over a few complicated issues. They'd work it out.

"Shall we go home or hit a club?" Andy asked as they entered their suburb on the outskirts of the CBD. The streets, normally buzzing with traffic and people, were quiet. All the shops were closed, as were the pubs and clubs they passed. A few youths staggered along the footpath.

"Where could we go? Looks like everything is shut."

"*The Ark*'s open today."

Simon frowned. "Are you sure about that?"

"Yep. I looked it up."

"Let's go, then. I don't feel like going home." It was easier to get drunk and party the night away than face his conscience.

CHAPTER 7

*N*atalie found Adam in the cafeteria. Two polystyrene cups were filled with coffee, and he was pouring sugar into them from the tubes in the dish on the side board. She sidled up to him and slipped her arms around his waist. "Hello you."

He turned his head and smiled at her. "This is a nice surprise. Did you leave Elysha alone?"

Natalie shook her head. "Mum and Bruce are with her."

"Oh, right." He sighed with resignation. Since Colin Daley had turned up claiming he was Elysha's father, Natalie had not wanted to let her out of her sight, even choosing to stay overnight with her. Adam said she was being paranoid. *'He's not going to steal her,'* he'd said countless times, but he hadn't convinced her.

She stepped aside, took a cup, and headed to a table beside the window. Adam joined her and sat opposite. She took a sip, set the cup down and sighed. "This isn't how I imagined we'd be spending Christmas day."

"Me either." His voice was clipped.

Natalie narrowed her eyes. "We can't leave her alone."

"We can't stay here twenty-four seven." He held her gaze.

Natalie pursed her lips, her steady gaze not wavering. "I don't trust him."

Adam shook his head and ran his hand through his hair. She hated seeing him frustrated with her. He was normally the peacemaker. He could calm a classroom of aggressive teenage boys. He remained calm in the face of almost everything, but he was annoyed with her because she didn't trust Colin Daley when he apparently did.

"Are you going to stay all night again? It's Christmas," he said.

"Yes."

"They've got security, you know."

She felt the nauseating sinking of despair. "I'm just so worried, Adam. We can't lose her now."

He reached out and took her hand. "We won't, sweetheart. It'll be fine, you'll see."

She sniffed and tried to stop her lip from trembling. "I'm sorry. I can't help it. If anything happened to her, I don't think I could forgive myself."

He rubbed her hand softly. "I know, but I truly doubt we'll see him again."

"You're always so positive. I got the feeling he was serious about wanting her."

"If he is, we'll take him to court."

"There's no guarantee we'd win."

"No, but we'd have to trust the system to do what's best for Elysha."

"What if they thought she's better off with her biological father than she is with us?" she asked pointedly.

Their gazes locked. She sensed that Adam finally understood her fear. Since they were both teachers, they'd witnessed countless custody battles over the years. The mother usually won, but with Paige deceased, the court could easily grant custody to Elysha's father, and not to them, should it go that far.

Adam swallowed hard. "I hadn't considered that."

"We know how it can go, Adam. This is serious. We could lose her."

"We'll just have to pray. There's not a lot else we can do."

"Yes. But I also want to stay." She picked up her coffee and took a sip.

"Okay. You win."

She smiled. "I knew you'd understand."

"It *would* be terrible to lose her."

"I can't imagine it."

"No, neither can I. Let's pray about it now."

Natalie glanced around. Maybe because it was Christmas the place wasn't busy. Only one other woman sat a table on her own. Not that it mattered. They shouldn't be embarrassed about praying in public, but it did seem strange. She turned and faced him. "Good idea."

They joined hands and bowed their heads. Adam began. "Lord God, we bring this situation before You. Despite the sad circumstances of Paige's death, we're so thankful for the opportunity to be parents to Elysha. We already love her so much. We ask now that You go before us and smooth the way forward. We don't know what Colin Daley is thinking, but You do, Lord. We appreciate that learning he might be Elysha's father would have come as a shock to him, but from what we know, he doesn't seem like the type of father she needs, and it would grieve our hearts greatly if she went to him. Please let him step aside and do what's right for Elysha. In Jesus' precious name. Amen."

Natalie cleared her throat. "Lord, I can't imagine the pain of losing Elysha now. You know how much we long to be her parents. How much we want to shower her with love and to teach her Your ways. Lord, please help us through this. If Colin Daley is her father, please let him willingly step aside without a fuss. And bless dear little Elysha. Thank You that she's making great progress and will be coming home soon. In Jesus' precious name. Amen."

Adam squeezed her hand and looked up. "Let's go and see her."

"Yes." Natale smiled as she stood and finished her coffee. After tossing the empty cup into the bin, she slipped her arm around Adam's waist and leaned in close as he placed his arm around her shoulder, and together they walked back to the ward.

Her mum was still holding Elysha when they reached the nursery. She looked up and smiled. Bruce was sitting in a chair reading a magazine which he closed when they entered.

"How has she been?" Natalie whispered.

"A perfect little angel," Mum replied, looking down at Elysha with a proud smile on her face.

"She's such a good little girl." Natalie's heart burst with love as she trailed the tip of her finger down Elysha's cheek.

"You were quick. I thought you'd be longer."

Natalie flashed a glance at Adam. "We…we were wanting to confirm with the nurse that I'll be staying with her again tonight."

Mum frowned. "On Christmas night? Is that really necessary?"

"We think so. We don't trust Colin Daley."

"Well, off you go. We're fine with her."

"Okay. Thank you. We won't be long." Natalie took Adam's hand and they headed to the nurse's station. The whole ward was covered with Christmas decorations. Brightly coloured tinsel criss-crossed the corridors, and a large Christmas tree, complete with baubles and flashing lights, sat opposite the nurse's station. A multitude of Christmas cards covered the counter, no doubt sent by parents who'd also spent the first weeks of their babies' lives in this very ward.

The duty nurse, a young woman with ginger hair and a cheerful smile looked up as they approached. "Can I help you?"

"We're just confirming that Natalie will be staying with Elysha again tonight. There's no problem with that is there?" Adam's tone was very polite and non-demanding.

The nurse hesitated. "I'll need to check, but I can't see there'd be any problem."

"Thank you. We'd appreciate that very much."

"We know you're concerned about Mr. Daley, but there isn't any way he could walk out with Elysha."

"We know the hospital is secure, but there's always a first time for everything."

"You could be right, although I think it's highly unlikely. I'll speak with Admin and will let you know."

Adam smiled again. "Thank you."

The nurse found them an hour later while they were eating Christmas dinner with Mum and Bruce and advised them that there was no problem with Natalie staying overnight with Elysha.

Natalie smiled and thanked her. They'd done as much as they could to fast-track the adoption process, but Christmas had come and the court was closed. The earliest date they'd get an answer was the first week in January. The prospect of staying in the hospital until then made her feel tired, but it was something she believed strongly she should do. She didn't trust Colin Daley one bit.

CHAPTER 8

The following week passed slowly. Much to Natalie's relief, Adam agreed to share the load with her and they took it in turns to stay overnight with Elysha. Wendy and Bruce took a week's vacation at the beach. They'd booked the apartment at Avoca on the Central Coast just north of Sydney when they'd expected his family to be coming for Christmas. They were going to cancel the booking, but Natalie and Adam encouraged them to go. "A change of scenery will do you good, Mum. Go," Natalie had told her on Christmas night while they were having dinner together.

Natalie had also begun to believe that Colin Daley might have lost interest in Elysha and she grew ever hopeful that one day soon their adoption would be made official. Elysha had gained weight and was feeding well, and since they'd been granted temporary custody early on, they looked forward to bringing her home as soon as the doctor said she was ready to be released.

All that changed on January third when Natalie opened the letterbox after arriving home from her day at the hospital. Her face lit up as she pulled out the official envelope bearing the insignia of the Family Court. She opened it eagerly, expecting it to be the official notification of their adoption. Her eyes enlarged as she read the letter.

We're sorry to inform you that your adoption application is being challenged, and that Elysha Grace Miller will be released to the care of a foster family in the short term. Due to the sensitive nature of the case, you will not be granted access until the official court orders have been issued.

Natalie's knees buckled and she barely made it to the couch before dropping in a heap. This couldn't be happening. No one had told them that Colin Daley was officially challenging their application. They didn't even know he'd had his DNA test. Deep gutteral weeping erupted from within her. After getting her emotions under control, she calmed enough to call Adam.

Speed-dialing his number, she waited for him to answer. "Adam…"

"I know." He sounded devastated. "She's gone. I didn't know how to tell you. I'm on my way home."

"How can they do this? Take her like that? It's not right."

"I don't know. We'll have to fight for her."

"It should have been a simple process."

"It was. Until Colin Daley turned up."

"Maybe we should go and see him."

"I don't think that's a good idea."

"Why not?"

"We don't know what he's like, Nat."

"But we have to do something." She began to sob again.

"We have to pray. Trust God."

"I know. But I feel helpless."

"That's often when He can do His best work. When we have to rely on Him totally and not on ourselves."

She drew a deep breath and reached for calm. "I'm sorry, Adam. It's just a huge shock. I'd better call Mum and tell her."

"Don't ruin their holiday, Nat. Wait until they come home. Or until we know more."

"I'll call the lawyer, then. See what she says."

"Good idea. But Nat, take a deep breath and gather your wits before you do."

"I already have. Now, I'm just mad."

"Okay. We'll get through this, sweetheart. I love you."

"I love you too." She ended the call and closed her eyes. Already, she felt an acute sense of loss so strong it was a physical pain in her gut. She swallowed the despair creeping up her throat and bowed her head. "Lord God," tears blinded her eyes and choked her voice, "we have to trust You to work this out. You know how devastated we are. Take care of our little girl. Let whoever's looking after her be kind to her and show her love." She yielded to convulsive sobs as she pictured Elysha going home with a complete stranger. *How could the court even think this was in Elysha's best interest?* She should have been coming home with her and Adam. "God, I'm sorry. Please help me to trust You." She pounded her fist on the back of the couch and buried her face in a cushion.

Sometime later, she opened her eyes, reached for a tissue and blew her nose. She stood and poured herself a glass of water. Calm. She needed to be calm. She drank the water, drew a steadying breath and called the lawyer. "Miranda. It's Natalie…"

S ɪ x ᴛ ʏ ᴍ ɪ ʟ ᴇ s away at Avoca Beach, Wendy and Bruce wandered along the water's edge, dodging waves as they lapped the shore. They'd had a lovely few days, and Wendy was glad they'd decided to come, although it was hard leaving Natalie and Adam when their adoption application was still pending. But Natalie had assured her she'd call if anything changed.

The sun shone on her back, warming her body and soul. It was marvellous how God used sunshine and sea to help heal a grieving heart. Not that she was over Paige's death. She never would be, but the intense grief she'd initially felt was slowly lifting and had been replaced by a dull ache instead.

Over the past few days, she and Bruce had caught up on sleep, taken long walks along the beach, and eaten out at a variety of restaurants. They'd also relaxed on the balcony of their apartment sipping coffee and reading, while occasionally glancing at the sparkling ocean in the distance. As uncomfortable as it felt, they'd invited Simon and Andy to visit. She felt a pang of guilt at her relief when they declined.

"I still don't know how to handle their relationship," she'd said to Bruce after putting the phone down.

Bruce took her hand and kissed it. "For someone who doesn't know how to handle it, you're handling it very well, my darlin'."

She chuckled. "You're always so encouraging. Thank you."

His eyes twinkled. "Thank *you*."

Now, Natalie and Adam were on her mind. "They should have heard by now," she said to Bruce as they walked hand in hand along the beach. "I think I'll call them when we get back to the unit."

"They said they'd call if anything changed."

"I know. But I just have this sense that something's happened."

"Well, call them if you're concerned. It can't hurt."

"I will. But let's get an ice cream first."

"I won't argue with that." Stopping, he pulled her into his arms and gazed into her eyes. "I love you, Wendy." He brushed hair off her forehead with his fingers, and her heart pounded as he lowered his mouth and kissed her slowly. Time stood still, and for a moment she forgot about Paige, about Simon, and about Natalie.

Sometime later, when they were back in the apartment, she sat on the balcony and called Natalie. She immediately knew something was wrong when Adam, not Natalie, answered. "Wendy. How are you?" He sounded tense. Not his normal, controlled self.

"I'm good. How are you and Natalie?"

She waited for his answer, her heart racing. Silence weighed heavily before he spoke again. "In shock. Elysha's been given to a foster family."

Wendy fell back against the chair and gripped her chest. "I can't believe it."

"Neither can we, but Colin Daley's challenging our adoption application. His DNA test has confirmed that he *is* the father, and they've sent Elysha into foster care until it gets sorted."

"Natalie must be devastated."

"She is. She's just gotten off the phone to our lawyer. A date hasn't been set for the case to be heard yet."

"We'll come back tonight. I need to be there for Natalie."

"She'd like that. She can't stop crying."

"My poor baby. Her heart must be breaking."

"It is."

"And so must yours."

He sniffed. "I'm doing all right."

"It doesn't sound that way."

"I'm as shocked as Natalie. I'm just holding it together a little better." His voice was jagged.

"Like you always do. You're a strong man, Adam. Look after her until we get there."

"I will. Drive carefully. And sorry for cutting your holiday short. We weren't going to tell you until you came back."

"We needed to know. This is a life-changing moment. For everyone."

"Especially for Elysha."

Wendy gulped. Elysha's life would be totally different if she went to live with Colin Daley. "We'll be there as soon as we can."

"Thank you, Wendy. We appreciate it."

"You're welcome. Give Natalie a hug from me."

"I will."

Wendy ended the call and stared at the ocean. Where was the justice? Natalie and Adam didn't deserve this. They would be wonderful parents to Elysha if they were given the chance. Tears spilled down her cheeks. *God, where are You in this? How could You have allowed this to happen? It's not what Paige would have wanted for her baby.* She covered her face with her hands and burst into tears.

A light hand rested on her shoulder. She reached up and covered it with hers.

"Don't give up hope, darlin'. God has a plan, even if we can't see what it is yet."

She nodded and brushed away her tears. She knew that, but it was hard to be positive when her heart was in tatters.

CHAPTER 9

*T*he return drive to Sydney seemed to take forever. A heavy invisible weight crushed Wendy's shoulders —she couldn't imagine how Natalie was feeling and she longed to hold and comfort her. Darkness was falling by the time Bruce stopped the car in front of Natalie and Adam's recently renovated home in the affluent suburb of Mossman on Sydney's north shore.

He switched the engine off and they climbed out. Wendy stretched and inhaled slowly. She wanted to be strong for Natalie, but she was fighting her own inner turmoil. She'd been so certain that their adoption application would process smoothly. That there'd be no hiccups. But now it was likely the court would grant custody to Colin Daley. He was her father, after all.

Bruce rounded the car, placed his hand on her shoulder and squeezed it. He'd been her rock. Her support. He maintained confidence that God had it under control. She tried to believe him.

"Are you ready?" he asked.

She nodded. Together, they walked along the pathway bordered with lavender to the front door. The house was an older style home that had been modernised but still held its old-world charm. Not that Wendy noticed it now. She was about to knock when Natalie opened the door. Her eyes were red and she looked distressed. Wendy stepped forward and enfolded her in her arms. Natalie sobbed against her shoulder.

Finally, her sobs eased and she apologised.

"You have nothing to be sorry for, sweetheart." Wendy drew a slow breath and prayed for strength.

"Come in."

She held Natalie's gaze for a moment and then followed her inside.

They stopped when they reached the kitchen. "Have you had dinner?" Natalie's voice was almost robotic.

Wendy shook her head. "No. But I'm not hungry."

"Neither am I."

"A cup of tea would be nice. Let me make it. Sit down, sweetheart." As Wendy filled the kettle and turned it on, inner strength surged through her. She could do this. With God, all things were possible.

THE FOUR ADULTS sat around the kitchen table, the conversation subdued. Nothing could be done until the following day. The lawyer had assured Natalie she'd do her best, but prepared her for the worst. "He's Elysha's father. The court will most likely grant him custody unless they perceive she's at risk."

"What do we know about him?" Bruce asked quietly.

"Very little," Adam replied. "I glimpsed him when he came to the hospital one day. He looked normal enough."

"Simon doesn't like him," Wendy said.

Natalie's head shot up. "I didn't know they knew each other."

"I don't know how well acquainted they are, but Simon met him when he and Paige were together," Wendy replied.

"Should we ask Simon to talk with him?" Natalie asked, her expression hopeful.

Adam leaned forward and placed his hand over Natalie's. He looked at her with tenderness. "We need to take the emotion out of this. Think clearly. Make good decisions. Pray about it. We don't want to do anything that might jeopardise our case." Adam had always been sensible. The love he and Natalie shared warmed Wendy's heart. They were such a steady, solid couple and she had no doubt they'd get through this, and even come out stronger. But she couldn't help but pray that they'd be granted custody of Elysha. Being unable to conceive naturally, adopting Paige's baby had seemed to be God ordained. *But now?* Was this just a hurdle? A test of their faith? Would they reflect Jesus in their actions and their thoughts? Would they be found worthy of their calling they'd received as God's people? Could they be humble and gentle now that they were faced with this strife?

Natalie nodded, her eyes moistening. "You're right. I'm clutching at straws. Let's pray about it."

"It's the only thing we can do that will make a difference," Adam said.

Wendy caught Bruce's gaze. Yes, it was the only thing. They needed direction. They needed peace. They needed God.

Joining hands and bowing their heads, they committed the situation to God once again and asked Him to grant them patience, wisdom, grace and humility. They also prayed for Elysha's protection, physically and spiritually. She'd been through so much in her short life, but God loved her and was looking after her, even if they had no idea where she was.

COLIN DALEY WHISTLED as he made his way along the footpath in downtown Kings Cross. On his way home from his day shift at *The Ark*, he stopped at the florist and bought a bunch of flowers.

"Celebrating something special?" the young female shop assistant asked as she wrapped the bunch in tissue paper.

"You could say that. I just found out that I'm a dad."

"Congratulations! A boy or a girl?"

"A girl." He couldn't wipe the smile off his face. Nor could he wait to hold his baby. When he'd seen Paige's sister holding her just the other day, he'd wanted to confront her there and then and tell her that Elysha was his. But it was better this way. He'd bided his time and now he had proof. DNA didn't lie. Now, all he had to do was convince Annie that this was a good idea, and Elysha would be theirs.

"There you go." The shop assistant handed him the bunch of flowers. "Enjoy parenthood!"

"I fully intend to."

Continuing on, he smiled at all he passed. This was a good day. He'd never thought about having children before, but when he heard that Paige Miller was pregnant, he'd begun to wonder if he was the father, and the idea had grown on him. Working at *The Ark*, he'd seen her brother on several occasions when he'd come in with his partner and he'd listened to their conversations discreetly while serving them beer. The more he heard, the more he was convinced he was the baby's father. He was planning to confront Paige when he heard that she'd died. It annoyed him that she hadn't told him about the baby. His smile slipped. He'd discovered that she hadn't stated who the father was on any of her medical documentation, but the DNA test proved it was him. He and Annie would be good parents. Not that they knew anything about raising babies, but how hard could it be?

Everyone he passed seemed happy today, but maybe it was just him. He continued whistling until he reached the front of the apartment building he and Annie lived in. The same one he and Paige had lived in until he gave her marching orders. She hadn't been happy when he'd brought Annie home to share their lives. She was so narrow minded and old-fashioned. He'd tried to get her to expand her thinking, explore different beliefs, try different things, but her Christian upbringing held her back. She couldn't cope with competition. A pity, because she was a nice girl.

He ran up the three flights of steps, ignoring the graffiti on the walls and the rubbish lying in the corners of the stairwell and pushed open the door. "Annie, I'm home!"

Annika Sorrensen appeared from the back bedroom

wearing only a long black T-shirt. A Scandinavian beauty, she'd dyed her long, blonde hair pitch black when she took on a Goth lifestyle and now had a uniquely seductive appearance. Colin had fallen for her the moment he'd met her at a fellow Goth's party almost a year ago.

Hiding the flowers behind his back, he stepped towards her.

She looked puzzled and tried to see behind him. "What have you got there?"

He laughed. "Flowers!" He whipped the bunch out and handed them to her.

She grew even more puzzled. "What for? You've never brought flowers before."

"I've got a surprise."

She angled her head and frowned. "Go on."

Suddenly, he grew tongue-tied. What if she didn't like the idea? The elation he'd felt after hearing the news deserted him and instead, he felt deflated.

"What's the matter?" She sidled up to him and fluttered her eyelashes.

He gazed at her. He'd never tire of Annie, but he sensed that his news might not please her. But he needed to tell her.

"Annie." He rubbed her arms. "We're going to be parents."

Her dark brows drew together. "What do you mean?"

"Paige had a baby and I'm the father."

She stepped back. "How do you know? Anyone could be the father the way she carried on after she left."

"I had a DNA test done."

"What? Why would you do that?" Colin was surprised the overhead light didn't break with the shrillness of her voice.

"Because I wanted to know for sure. And…and because I want her."

"The baby?" She looked incredulous.

He nodded.

"How? Why would you get her?"

"Because Paige died," he replied quietly. Although he'd told her to leave, he had loved her at one time and felt bad that she'd passed away.

"I didn't know. I'm sorry." Annie's voice softened. "Where's the baby?"

"In care, for now."

She held his gaze. He didn't know what she was thinking. His heart raced.

"And you want me to help you look after her?"

He nodded slowly. Moments passed. And then she slapped him. "In your dreams! I'm not looking after someone else's baby."

"Annie. Don't be like that. You should see her. She's beautiful. So tiny. So defenseless." His shoulders fell. "Motherless."

She pushed him away. "If you bring the baby here, I go. It's me or her." She folded her arms defiantly.

For the first time in many years, tears found their way to his eyes. "Annie, you don't mean that."

"I do. It's me or her."

He gulped. How could she do this to him? "Let's not make any hurried decisions. Come to bed." It was the only way he knew of getting through to her. He took her hand. She didn't resist. Maybe she'd see things in a different light later.

.   .   .

COLIN COULDN'T SLEEP. He got up and poured himself a drink of water. What was he doing? Why was he so determined to get Paige's baby?

Would he choose her over Annie?

He sat in the semi-darkness. Neon lights from the buildings across the road flickered, illuminating the room with garish colours. Sometimes he wondered what his life would have been like had his mother lived. Like Paige, she'd died in childbirth. He never knew his father. That was why he wanted Paige's baby. To protect her from what he'd been through. Foster home after foster home. Never belonging. He wanted his child to belong. To know who she was. He ignored the voice inside his head that told him she *was* wanted. The voice that told him he was being selfish. Paige's sister wanted her. He could see it in her face and in the way she looked at the baby. The way she held her. But if she and her husband adopted her, he'd never see Elysha. He couldn't allow that to happen.

But Annie didn't want her. His clenched his fists as his plans crashed around him.

$\mathcal{L}$ater that night, Wendy and Bruce returned home after leaving Natalie and Adam's place. Although nothing outwardly had changed, inside, Wendy felt more at peace. It seemed strange heading out of the city to go home. For so many years, she'd lived near the harbour, but now she and Bruce lived on a small farm on the edge of the city. It couldn't have been any more different, but it felt nice to be coming home to *their* home. She was looking forward to settling in properly. Making friends. It would take time, and she still wasn't ready. But she'd make a start. Soon.

Bruce flicked the high beam headlights as they turned into their road. It was so dark away from the city lights. Wendy was learning to like it, although sometimes it felt isolated. Like now. With everything that had happened, she would have liked to be closer to Natalie and Adam instead of almost an hour's drive away. Natalie would call in the morning after she'd spoken with the lawyer, and Wendy had assured her that she and Bruce were on hand for whatever.

"Are you okay, darlin'?" Bruce turned his head and looked at her.

She nodded. "Yes. I'm looking forward to bed."

"It's been a long day."

"It definitely has. I do hope the case gets heard quickly. I don't like the thought of Elysha being cared for by a stranger."

"I'm sure she's being well-looked after."

"I know, but it's not the same, is it?"

"No, but we have just to trust. And be patient."

"Yes, I know."

Bruce slowed and turned the car into their driveway. The house was set back from the road, and security lights came on as they approached. "It still doesn't seem quite like home, does it?" she asked.

"Home for me is where you are, my darling." He squeezed her hand.

She let out a small laugh. "You're such a romantic."

"Do you have a problem with that?"

She shook her head. "Not at all."

"Good."

The car came to a halt and they climbed out. Other than the occasional whinnying of a horse, most likely Prince, all was quiet. A neighbour had been looking after their animals while they'd been away, but no doubt Bruce's large black stallion was just as eager for a fast ride as he was.

"It's a lovely evening." Wendy stopped and gazed up at the star-studded sky as she sucked in a deep breath of the clean, country air.

Standing behind her, Bruce slipped his arms around her waist and nuzzled her neck.

Wendy leaned against him and relaxed. They were home.

SOMETIME DURING THE night Natalie had a dream that was so real she woke in a sweat, her chest heaving. It wasn't real, but the panic she'd felt was palpable.

Beside her, Adam stirred. "What is it, Nat? What's happened?" He sounded groggy as he wriggled up the bed.

"I had a dream..." She gulped and began panting.

"Elysha?"

Natalie nodded. "It was horrible. She was in somebody's arms. They were running away with her. And then she disappeared." Her breaths expelled in short, quick pants.

"It was only a dream, darling. It's not real." He pulled her close and hugged her.

"I know. I'm so scared of losing her, Adam."

He kissed the top of her head. "I know. It'll be okay, you'll see."

"I hope so." She burst into tears and sobbed into his chest.

He rocked her in his arms. "It'll be okay, Nat. Stay strong. Okay?"

Nodding, she sniffed and grabbed a tissue and then blew her nose.

"Hot chocolate?" He tucked a lock of hair behind her ear.

"Yes, please."

"Stay there, I'll make it."

"Thank you."

He flicked the lamp on and climbed out of bed. She glanced at the clock. Three a.m. Would Elysha be awake? Would she be wondering where she was? Who was holding her? Fresh tears welled in Natalie's eyes and rolled down her cheeks. It wasn't right. Elysha should have been here with them.

She slipped out of bed and padded to the nursery. Everything was ready. They'd repainted the room in soft pink, hung new curtains and colourful mobiles. The cot was made, the pram ready. The change-table drawers were filled with nappies and wipes. The only thing missing was Elysha. Natalie's gaze shifted to the picture frame with the printed Bible verse they'd chosen for her. Psalm 139, verse 14:

I praise You because I am fearfully and wonderfully made

Natalie sat in the rocking chair with one of the tiny vests they'd bought for Elysha clenched in her hands and closed her eyes. It was so hard to make sense of everything. Sorrow over not being able to conceive her own baby still weighed heavily on her heart, but that sorrow had been largely replaced with joy when Elysha was born, although that joy was tinged with grief. That Paige had to die so they could have a child... It reminded Natalie of the ultimate sacrifice Jesus had made for mankind. He gave His life so that all who believed could live. It wasn't the same, but in Natalie's highly emotional state, it all melded together.

I was with Elysha when she was conceived. Your sister might not have planned her, but I knew Elysha from the beginning, and I love her. I'll take care of her. I'll never leave her or forsake her.

Peace like she'd never known flooded Natalie's heart. *Oh*

God, thank You. Thank You for looking after my baby. Although tears streamed down her cheeks, her breathing slowly calmed, and when Adam entered soon after, she opened her eyes and gave him a weak smile.

"Here you are, Nat. Drink this." He handed her a mug filled with hot chocolate.

She took it gratefully. When she sipped it, the sweet liquid slid down her throat easily, warming her. Calming her. "Thank you. It's just what I needed."

"You're welcome." He smiled at her. "She'll be home one day soon. I'm sure of it."

And for the first time, she believed him.

CHAPTER 11

*W*hen Simon heard from his mother that Colin Daley had been confirmed as Elysha's father, he headed straight for *The Ark*. He doubted that Daley would be there, but it was a start. He should have known where the dude lived, but he didn't. Somewhere in Kings Cross was all he knew.

He and Andy had been at *The Ark* the previous evening until late and he didn't feel too good. He was drinking too much. He knew it, but how could he say no to Andy? He was persuasive in every way. Even with their wedding plans. The date had been set for March the first, and the invitations had been sent. Andy wasn't wasting a moment. Simon felt he was on an express train he couldn't get off.

He entered *The Ark* and ordered a Coke.

"Big night?" The bartender raised a brow.

Simon shrugged as he downed the glass. "Is Colin around?"

"No, mate. He doesn't start 'til late."

"Do you know where he lives?"

"Somewhere round here. Not sure where. Sorry." The bartender returned to washing glasses.

"No worries." Simon gave a backwards wave as he headed for the door. Stepping outside, he squinted and put on his sunglasses. Trying to find where Colin Daley lived would be like looking for a needle in a haystack, but he needed to find the dude. He had no right to Paige's baby. He quickly corrected himself. *Natalie's baby.*

He looked up the street, then down. He'd met Daley with Paige at the pub down the street where the Goths hung out so he headed that way. Although he was used to the Cross, this part of town made him uneasy. Narrow alleyways crisscrossed the main drag, bordered by buildings covered in graffiti. The stench of stale alcohol and urine filled his nostrils as he took a left and wandered down one of them. A drunk lay passed out with a bottle tucked under his arm, a mangy dog snarled from behind a rusty gate, and a woman he guessed was a prostitute from the way she was scantily dressed, batted her eyes at him as he walked by. He ignored her.

He finally reached a door he recognised. The black sign swinging above it confirmed it was a bar called *Devilles*. Pushing it open, he entered a dark hallway lit only with dim wall sconces. The hall led to a large room which was also dim and filled with a haze that seemed much like fog. Dark music played from the speakers. He was surprised to see a number of figures lounging around. He thought Goths mainly came out at night. Maybe these were left-overs. None of them appeared to be Daley, though it was hard to tell in the feeble light. He walked to the bar, hands deep in his pockets. A young pale-faced woman with long, dark hair and heavy make-up glanced up. "Can I help you?"

"I'm looking for Colin Daley. Do you know where I can find him?"

"Who's asking?"

"Simon. Simon Miller."

Her face grew even paler, if that were possible. "Haven't seen him here for ages. Sorry."

"But you know him?"

"You could say that."

"Do you know where he lives?"

"I couldn't tell you even if I knew. Privacy laws."

"Can you give him a message?"

"Maybe."

"Tell him to leave our family alone, or..."

"Or what?"

"Or... he'll regret it." Simon cringed. He sounded pathetic. He hadn't planned this out. What was he going to do to the dude when he found him? Punch him? Ask him politely to leave them alone? To mind his business? Daley would laugh in his face.

"Okay. I'll tell him." Her amused expression made him cringe even further. Slinking away, he breathed a sigh of relief when he reached the outside. It was useless. He was useless. He couldn't even help his family. He was a failure in every way. Even with his work, he was a failure. He hadn't told his mum, but just before Christmas he'd been let go from his job. He thought he'd been doing well as the area manager for a fast food chain, but it seemed not. Andy had told him not to worry about it. He'd find another job. In the meantime, Andy was working, so there wasn't a problem. But Simon didn't want to be looked after by Andy. He wanted to pull his weight. To be someone of worth. He may as well get drunk, since he had nothing better to do.

You are precious and honored in my sight. I have loved you with an everlasting love; I have drawn you with unfailing kindness.

Simon shook his head. *No. Don't do that to me, God. I'm not listening.*

For you know that it was not with perishable things such as silver or gold that you were redeemed from the empty way of life handed down to you from your ancestors, but with the precious blood of Christ, a lamb without blemish or defect.

I don't want to hear it. Covering his ears, he raced for the nearest bar and ordered two double scotches. He downed them and ordered another. Not until his mind was numb did he stop.

CHAPTER 12

*A*fter spending an hour immersed in her Bible while Bruce was riding Prince, Wendy finished unpacking and prepared breakfast. While waiting for Bruce to return, she grabbed a hat, slipped on her sandals and headed to the letterbox. Arriving late the previous night, they hadn't stopped to empty it on the way in.

The sun was warm on her back and it promised to be another glorious day, the type that made you want to pack a picnic and head to the beach. But they were a long way from the beach now, so a day beside the pool would have to suffice. Unless, of course, Natalie needed them. Wendy had decided to be patient and to wait until Natalie called her, but it was such a challenge not to call for an update. Natalie would let her know as soon as she knew anything, of that she was sure.

She reached the letterbox and took out a handful of mail. Junk mail, a few bills, and a fancy envelope, probably containing a belated Christmas card. She placed the mail into her cloth bag and wandered back to the house, stopping to pick a few flowers on the way.

She poured herself a cup of coffee, sat at the table, and opened the mail. She chose the fancy one first. It wasn't a Christmas card; it was an invitation. A wedding invitation. Her mouth fell open at reading the names of the intended...*Simon Miller and Andrew Lamond.*

Wendy was speechless. She'd been so convinced that Simon wouldn't go through with a wedding. How could he? How could he go against what he knew was right? She drew a slow breath. She couldn't go. Shaking her head, she willed herself not to succumb to tears. She'd shed too many already. *God, I don't understand, I truly don't.* Closing her eyes, she sought solace from the passages she'd read that morning. It was the story of Abraham and Sarah, who'd longed all their life for a baby, and then, when they were past their child-bearing years, God had blessed them with Isaac. The story had given her comfort when she read it, but now that her faith was being challenged yet again, could she truly trust God to answer her prayers?

It would be great to speak with someone who had a gay child. Someone who had experienced the same emotions and questions, and who could offer guidance and encouragement. *Elizabeth!* Of course! Greg's grandmother in London had had a son, Graham, who was a homosexual. He'd died of AIDS not long before Greg passed away. Although elderly, she'd be the perfect person to speak with. Wendy checked the time and did the conversion. Seven a.m. Sydney, eight p.m. London. Elizabeth should be awake.

Standing, she walked to the study and looked up Elizabeth's

number. She'd recently moved from her stately manor home on the outskirts of London, into a care facility. Wendy waited patiently for her to answer. When she did, her voice was frailer than when they'd last spoken, but her mind still seemed as sharp. "Wendy! How lovely to hear your voice. How are you? And how's that cowboy of yours?"

A smile came to Wendy's lips. When Bruce accompanied her to Elizabeth's birthday party in London not long after they met, he almost stole the show. Elizabeth had warmed to him and even encouraged her to pursue their relationship. Wendy was so glad she had. "He's great, Elizabeth. Thank you for asking." She drew a calming breath. Not only did Elizabeth not know about Simon, as far as she knew, she didn't know about Paige's death, either. "Have you got time for a chat?"

"I've got all the time in the world for you, my dear."

"Thank you." Tears sprang to Wendy's eyes as she told Elizabeth about Paige and baby Elysha. And about how excited Natalie and Adam were about the prospect of becoming parents despite the circumstance. She mentioned that their adoption application was still processing, although it had been delayed. There was no reason to tell her about Colin Daley.

"God has a wonderful way of bringing good out of bad. I'm sure it will work out," Elizabeth said.

"So am I." Wendy paused. "But that wasn't the main reason for my phone call."

"What is it, dear? Not problems with Bruce?"

"No. Not at all. He's wonderful. No, it's Simon. We found out recently that he's gay. But not just that. He's planning on marrying his partner." Wendy's voice caught. She could barely bring herself to utter the words. They were distasteful in her mouth. But this was her son they were talking about. She felt so mixed up. Confused.

"Oh." Elizabeth's voice grew serious. "How are you handling the news?"

"Not too well, I'm afraid. I was hoping you could give me some guidance."

"I'll certainly try. It's a shock when something like this hits so close to home, but I certainly understand how you're feeling. When Graham told us, William and I had no idea what to say to our friends or family, let alone him. We asked him to keep it quiet. We were embarrassed and upset. Disappointed. We almost disowned him."

"Did that ever change?"

"Yes. William and I discussed it at length, and we prayed about it. We both strongly believed that homosexuality was a sin, that it wasn't what God intended, but we reminded ourselves that Graham was created in God's image, and that helped us in the way we looked at him after learning about his sexuality.

"We tried not to look at the sin, because however much that image might be marred, Graham was still God's precious creation, so we tried to look beyond his homosexuality and instead see the God-like beauty in his life. We're all broken people, tarred with sin, and homosexuality is just another manifestation of that. At least, that's what I was taught and believe."

Wendy's heart quickened. It was exactly what she believed, too.

"It's not our role to convict others of their sin or to convert them. That's God's job. We're expected to love and to pray, and to live our lives in such a way that they might see God's grace in our lives. That doesn't mean we should relax our beliefs, though. Not at all. We should state what we believe, but do so with grace and love. The Christian view on homosexuality isn't a popular one. It's considered old-fashioned, but Christianity has always been counter-cultural, even in Jesus' day. Our biggest challenge is to respond with compassion and love while we hold our beliefs firm, and wait for God to act in their lives, just like we do with anyone else."

"I'm so glad I called you. That helps so much. But what should I do about the wedding?"

"Oh, my dear. I can't tell you what you should do. Graham never married his partner, I guess because it wasn't legal back then. But my view is that marriage is between a man and a woman, not two men or two women. Once again, that's not a popular view, but I believe it's a Biblical one. You'll need to pray about it, my dear. Hopefully, Simon will understand if you say you can't attend, but I'm sure he'll appreciate it if you do."

Wendy groaned. That wasn't what she wanted to hear. But Elizabeth was right. It wasn't up to her to say whether she should go or not. That was Wendy's decision. "Thank you so much, Elizabeth. It's been really helpful speaking with you. I've felt so alone in this."

"I understand. Being a Christian parent of a homosexual child can be a lonely experience, and can be very isolating if you let it. Just keep the lines of communication with Simon open, but don't be afraid to state your views. I'm sure he'll respect you more if you do."

"Did Graham ever turn away from his homosexuality and turn to God?"

"Not that I know of, but I don't know what was in his heart. I trust that he made peace with God before he died, but I don't know. Graham and his partner were together for many years. His partner was a good man and they had a respectful and loving relationship as far as I know, but I never gave up hope of him turning to God. And don't you give up, Wendy. You don't know what's going on inside Simon's heart."

"You're right. I'm so grateful that Paige turned back to God before she died. He was working on her without us knowing."

"Exactly. We're called to be faithful. To pray. To love. To display the fruit of the Spirit in our lives, and to leave the rest to God. Can I pray for you, my dear?"

"That would be wonderful, Elizabeth. Thank you."

Elizabeth cleared her throat. "Lord God, be with my dear Wendy. Help her see Simon and his partner the way You see them, as precious children made in Your image. Help her to look beyond their homosexuality and to see them as people seeking to find their way in this world. May they seek Your way, dear Lord. Work in their lives and draw them to Yourself. Convict them of their need of You, just as You have convicted us of our own need. We thank You for the gift of love that Jesus showed when He gave up all He had to come to earth to redeem broken mankind. For that we are ever grateful. Bless Wendy now, dear Lord. Let her experience Your peace and comfort in the face of her loss, and give her strength and wisdom as she deals with this new situation. Wrap Your arms around her. In Jesus' precious name. Amen."

"Amen." Wendy wiped tears from her eyes. "Thank you so much."

"You're more than welcome. Enjoy that new little grand-daughter of yours. And give my love to your cowboy."

Wendy chuckled. "I will. For sure. Thank you once again." She ended the call but remained pensive. Elizabeth's prayer had touched her heart, and her wise words had challenged her beliefs. Could she truly look beyond Simon and Andy's homo-sexuality and see them as God saw them? Could she react with grace instead of judgment and condemnation? She could, but only with God's help. If left to her natural self, she could easily react badly.

She closed her eyes as she sat at the desk. "Lord God, please help me. Thank You for Elizabeth and her wisdom. Help me to love Simon and Andy and to respect their right to live how they choose, even if it goes against what I believe. Let my thoughts, words and deeds honour and glorify You, and may they see in me the love of Jesus, in whose precious name I pray. Amen."

"Amen." Bruce's quiet voice sounded from behind.

She turned around. "How long have you been there, my darling?"

"Only a few seconds."

"I was talking with Elizabeth."

He frowned. "Elizabeth?"

"Sorry. Greg's grandmother."

"Aha. Now I know who you mean. Was the conversation helpful?"

"Beyond helpful. She was wonderful. But she wouldn't tell

me what to do with this." Wendy held up the invitation and waved it.

Bruce's eyes widened. "Their wedding invitation?"

She nodded.

"Oh. You didn't think he'd go through with it."

"It seems he is." She held his gaze. "Elizabeth said to pray about whether we should go or not. It's all we can do, because I truly don't know."

"She's a wise lady."

"She is. And she told me to give you her love."

"Did she?" His eyes twinkled. "And how are you going to do that?"

Chuckling, she stood and wrapped her arms around his neck. "Like this." She pulled his head down so their lips touched.

"Hmm...I like this." He smiled and then proceeded to kiss her slowly.

CHAPTER 13

*a*fter three drinks, Simon had had enough. He needed to tell Andy he couldn't marry him. He had to stop being a wimp. If Andy truly loved him, he'd understand. If he didn't... Simon gulped. He didn't want to even think about what it would be like to be single and lonely. He'd have no trouble finding another partner, but he didn't want another partner. He wanted Andy. *So, why was he reluctant to get married?*

"Haven't you read ... that at the beginning the Creator 'made them male and female,' and said, 'For this reason a man will leave his father and mother and be united to his wife, and the two will become one flesh?"

He gritted his teeth. *I don't want to know...* Thumping his empty glass on the bartop, he strode outside hoping to rid his head of the noise, but pulled up short when he came face to face with Colin Daley.

"I believe you've been looking for me?" Daley flicked his long, dark hair over his shoulder and stared him down.

"Yes…" Simon drew himself up to his full five foot eleven inches.

"And?"

The guy was intimidating. Simon shrugged in defeat. "I made a mistake. Sorry." His voice slurred.

"Good. Mind your own business in future." Colin poked him in the chest and then walked off.

Simon seethed. It *was* his business. The baby was his niece. Striding after him, he called out, "Daley!"

The dude turned and sauntered to him. "What?"

"Paige didn't want you to know about the baby. She didn't want you to have anything to do with her."

"And how do you know that?"

"I just do. Do the right thing and let my other sister have her."

"She should be with her father. That's the right thing."

"Not when the father is you. You're low life." Spittle flew out of Simon's mouth as he spat the words.

"Like you can talk. Queer." Colin poked him in the chest against.

Before Simon could stop himself, he swung his fist and punched Colin Daley in the face, knocking him flying. It felt good. He followed with another punch, and another, until someone pulled him away. "Whoa, mate. You'll kill him."

"Good!"

"You don't mean that."

"Yeah, I do."

The man put his hands on his shoulders. "Come away before the police arrive."

Police? What have I done? He looked at Colin Daley's blood-covered face. He could easily have killed him if the stranger hadn't stopped him. What would he have said to Mum?

He allowed the man to lead him away. His head swam and he wasn't sure where they were going, but when they arrived in a small room underneath a building, the man gave him coffee and attended to his bruised and bloodied hands. "You sure gave him a good go."

"He deserved it."

"Want to talk about it?" the man asked gently.

"Not really."

"It might help. I'm Ellis, by the way. Ellis Gibson. And you are?"

"Simon Miller."

"Nice to meet you, Simon."

Simon grunted and studied the man. A shadow of a beard gave him a rugged appearance, at odds with his gentle voice. He wondered immediately if Ellis was hitting on him, but somehow, he didn't get that impression. If he wasn't, why was he paying him so much attention? "Why did you bring me here?"

"You needed help."

"I'm fine."

"Are you sure about that?" Ellis raised a brow as he placed a blood-stained wipe into the bin.

"Yes."

"If that's the case, why were you beating that guy to a pulp?"

Simon sucked in a breath. He hadn't meant to do that. He'd only intended to ask Daley to reconsider what he was doing with Elysha. Something had taken hold of him and he'd lost it. He shrugged. "I don't know." Defeat sounded in his voice.

"Seems to me you've got a lot going on in there." Ellis pointed to Simon's heart.

Simon initially denied it, but then nodded his head as tears stung his eyes. "You might be right."

"I've got as long as you need." Ellis sat down on a plastic chair and crossed his legs.

Frowning, Simon glanced around at the surroundings, a smallish area furnished simply with a plastic table and four chairs, and a very basic kitchenette. "Where am I?"

"The Emmaus Chapel. I'm a counsellor here."

Simon groaned and closed his eyes. How had he ended up in a chapel of all places? He'd heard about this place. Even considered coming in on several occasions, but he'd always walked on. Gays weren't welcome in a place like this.

"It's okay. I'm not going to preach at you. Do you want something to eat?" Ellis stood and washed his hands.

"What have you got?"

He opened the half-sized fridge and peered inside. "Not much, I'm afraid. A couple of sandwiches, a few pieces of left-over pizza, and a dodgy looking something or other that I think I'd give a miss." He pulled out a container of what appeared to be month-old takeout and tossed it in the bin.

"Pizza sounds good."

"No problem." Pulling out several slices, he placed them in the microwave. "Do you live around here?"

"Ten minutes away."

"What do you do?"

Simon's shoulders fell. "I'm between jobs at the moment."

"That's no good. I'm sure you'll find something soon."

"I hope so."

The microwave dinged. Ellis pulled the pizza out, placed two pieces on a plate and set it on the table in front of Simon. He put the other piece on another plate and sat beside him.

The smell of the pizza made Simon realise how hungry he was and he demolished the first slice in a matter of seconds.

"Good?"

He nodded. "Yeah. Thanks."

"You're welcome." Ellis leaned back in his chair and folded his arms, studying him. "What was going on with that guy?"

"It's a long story."

"Like I said, I've got all day."

Simon debated how much he should say as he savoured the second piece of pizza. In the end, he decided he had nothing to lose and told Ellis about Paige, how she'd gone off the rails after their dad died and got herself pregnant, how she died in childbirth and that his other sister and her husband were adopting the baby. How Colin Daley had discovered Elysha was his and was contesting the adoption. He didn't mention Andy.

"That's a lot of stuff going on. No wonder you were angry."

He shrugged. "Yeah. I lost it big time."

"Seems to me like you need some stress relief. Do you surf?"

"I used to." Simon had an instant flashback to the times when Dad took him to Bondi Beach and they hung out on boards for hours on end.

"Feel like catching some waves?"

"Now?"

"Why not?"

"I don't have any swim trunks."

"I've got spares. Come on." Ellis stood and opened a door that led into a hallway. From a cupboard, he pulled out a pair of brightly coloured boardshorts and a black rashguard and held them up. "I think they'll fit."

Simon hesitantly took them.

"You can get changed in the bathroom. Come out when you're ready." Ellis indicated a room further down the hallway.

Entering it, Simon closed the door, sat on the toilet and rested his elbows on his knees. What was he doing? Could he really go surfing with a stranger? *What would Andy think?* He checked the time on his watch. Andy's shift at the hospital would be finishing soon. He should go home. Tell Andy he wanted to call the wedding off. His pulse raced at the thought. Andy would be shocked and hurt. He could even end their relationship. Tonight, Simon could be single. No, he'd go for a surf. Some thinking time would be good. And besides, Ellis seemed like a cool dude, even though he was a Christian.

Standing, he changed out of his clothes and put on the swimwear Ellis had given him. They fit perfectly. He folded his clothes neatly and carried them back to the kitchen area. Ellis was already changed and handed him a bag to put his clothes in. "Bring them with you if you like."

Simon followed him down a narrow stairwell which led to the carpark. Ellis headed for an old white van and climbed into the driver's seat. Simon glanced around after settling into the passenger seat. Several surf boards filled the back of the van. "Do you surf a lot?"

"As often as I can. It's a great way to start the day."

Simon guessed it was. When he was working, he started

each day with a coffee to-go. Surfing sounded a lot more appealing.

Ellis started the van and headed into the traffic. "This is the worst part. But I guess it's like most things in life. You have to take the journey to reach your destination."

"You said you weren't going to preach."

"Sorry."

They drove in silence. Ten minutes later, the dazzling blue of the ocean came into view. Ellis parked the van, and after jumping out, opened the back door and pulled two boards out. "Let's go."

Simon tucked one of the boards under his arm and followed him. Being later in the day, only a few surfers were out. The waves were of moderate size, with just a few decent breaks. Simon lay on his board and began paddling. Within moments, his arms started to ache. Andy had been trying to get him to work out with him, and now he wished he had. He remembered the words Ellis had spoken and pushed on. He could do this. Soon, they reached the point where the other surfers sat waiting for the right wave. Ellis shifted to a sitting position and Simon followed suit.

The salty sea spray was cool on his face, the water fresh, but not cold, on his legs. Wispy clouds scudded across the sky, and seagulls soared effortlessly above. Ellis had been right—this was the perfect stress relief.

For several minutes, Simon sat, wishing he could stay bobbing up and down in the gentle rollers instead of chasing a ride, but he had no choice when Ellis called out, "Here's one, mate. Let's go."

He paddled frantically and soon he was riding the wave. It

had been many years since he'd stood on a board, but it came back easily. The exhilaration was beyond belief.

"Going back out?" Ellis asked as they both pulled out of the wave as it dissipated.

"Sure."

The next hour passed too quickly. The sun was low in the sky when they strolled back along the beach, heading for the showers. "How was that?" Ellis asked.

"It was great. Thanks for suggesting it."

"You're welcome. Come again in the morning if you like."

"I'll give it some thought."

Reaching the outdoor showers, they rinsed the salt and sand off themselves and the boards before heading back to the van.

"Would you like me to drop you home?"

Simon's shoulders fell. "I'm not sure I want to go home."

"Problems?"

"You could say that. I need to tell my boyfriend I don't want to get married."

"Oh."

"Did that surprise you?"

"Nothing surprises me, Simon. But it sounds like you're struggling with it."

He sighed heavily. *More than you think...* He shrugged and stared out the window.

"Want to talk about it?"

Simon blew out a breath and turned to face Ellis. "My conscience is getting at me. My Mum's a Christian."

"And you're not?"

"I used to believe."

"What changed?"

He shrugged again. "I'm not sure. I drifted away. It didn't seem relevant anymore."

"And now?"

"I don't know. I know God doesn't like gays."

"That's not true. He loves all people."

"That's not what they say in most churches."

"I can't vouch for what other churches say, but God doesn't withhold love from anyone."

"But He doesn't approve of what we do behind closed doors."

"That might be true, but that's between you and Him. We're all sinners."

Simon stared out the window as a memory verse from Sunday School came to mind... *for all have sinned and fall short of the glory of God.*

He gritted his teeth. *What are You trying to tell me, God?*

I did not send my Son into the world to condemn the world, but to save the world through Him.

"Do you think God can cure me of being gay?"

"I don't know, mate, but I know He has a cure for sin. If you accept that cure, He can sort everything else out in time."

That seemed a reasonable answer. Other than a miracle happening, Simon didn't expect God would change his nature overnight, if ever.

"Where should I take you?" Ellis asked. "If you'd rather not go home, there's a hostel near the chapel."

"I think I need to go home."

"Can I pray for you?"

Tears welled in Simon's eyes. "I'd like that."

Ellis pulled the van over and placed his hand on Simon's shoulder. "Lord God, I pray for my brother. Simon's heart is troubled. Let him know how much You love him. How precious he is to You. Help him to work through his issues and to be freed from the sin that binds us all. Lord, we know that only in You can we find the answers for all of life's problems. Only in You can we can find true peace. Bless him now and go with him. In Jesus' precious name. Amen."

Simon wiped his eyes. "Thank you."

"You're welcome. Now, if you give me your address, I'll drop you home."

Simon told him, and as Ellis stopped the van in front of his apartment block, Simon asked if he could go surfing again in the morning.

"Sure. Would you like me to pick you up?"

"I've got a car. I can meet you there."

"Too easy. I usually get there at six. See you then. Oh, and I'll be praying for you."

Simon smiled at his new friend. "Thank you."

Opening the door a few minutes later, Simon was relieved to find a note from Andy. "Been called back to work—not sure when I'll be home. I've left some catering brochures for you to look at. Love you, Andy xx."

CHAPTER 14

*N*atalie ran for the phone, hoping it was their lawyer, Miranda. She was pleased when it was.

"Natalie. I've got news. The case is scheduled for Thursday."

It was the best news she could have received. She and Adam had feared it might be weeks, or even months, before their case came before the court. Two days was unbelievable. No, not unbelievable. God was able to do immeasurably more than they could ever ask or imagine.

"That's wonderful. Thank you. Have...have you heard how Elysha is?" Thoughts of her baby were with her constantly. She felt so bereft as she battled the loneliness and heartache of an empty crib. She might not have given birth to Elysha, but in every other way, she was her mother.

"She's doing fine. The foster parents are wonderful."

Tears sprang to Natalie's eyes. "Thank you. Will she be there on Thursday?"

"No. I'm sorry."

"It's okay. I didn't expect she would be." She bit her lip to stop from crying. "What chance do we have?"

"I'm quietly confident. It depends on how well the other party presents himself."

"He's a Goth. How could they give him custody?" As soon as she said the words, she wished she could take them back. Being a Goth shouldn't preclude anyone from being a parent. "Sorry. I shouldn't have said that."

"It's okay. I understand your frustration. We'll do our best."

"Thanks Miranda. I appreciate it. See you on Thursday."

As soon as Natalie ended the call, she went into the study and gave Adam the news, then she called her mother. Both were overjoyed that it had been scheduled so soon.

"God is answering our prayers. I'm so thankful," she said to her mum.

"It seems that way, dear. But we need to keep our eyes focused on Him, not on what we want."

"You're right, Mum. It's so easy to get carried away by what we want and not seek what He wants. Although I sincerely pray they're the same thing."

"As do I, but we have to trust Him, regardless. I was reminded of that yet again this morning in my devotions."

"I don't know how I'll cope if Colin Daley is granted custody."

"Let's deal with that if it happens and not before."

"You're right. I think I need to do something to get my mind off everything for a while. All I think of here at home is Elysha. It doesn't help when her room is empty."

"Would you like to come for dinner?"

A smile grew on Natalie's face. "That would be nice. Thank

93

you."

"I'll see if Simon can come."

"And Andy?"

Her mother paused. "Yes. And Andy. I spoke to Greg's grandmother yesterday. It helped a lot."

"You'll have to tell me what she said. I have no idea what Adam and I should do about this wedding."

"I'm still not sure either. Elizabeth said to pray about it."

"What? The wedding, or whether to go?"

"Both."

"Good advice. I still can't get my head around it. Andy's a nice guy, but..."

"No need, darling, I understand."

"I expect you do. We'll get ready and come out."

"See you soon."

WENDY ENDED the call and breathed in and out with relief. It was such good news that the hearing was so soon. Her heart went out to Natalie and Adam. Going home without Elysha had to be soul-destroying, and yet, so many things in life were unfair, but each offered an opportunity for personal and spiritual growth. Seeking first the Kingdom was the key. Abiding in God. Trusting Him to work all things for His good. Not theirs. It was a lesson she was slowly learning.

She dialed Simon's number. She didn't like calling him during work hours, and he often didn't answer. This time, he did. She told him the news about the hearing and invited him and Andy to dinner.

He hesitated. "Um. Andy might be working, but I can come."

"Okay, darling, that's fine. See you about six?"

"Sure. What can I bring?"

"Just yourself. Come earlier if you want."

"Thank you. I'll see how the rest of my day goes."

After ending the call, Wendy put her mind towards dinner. What should she cook? It was still hot, so a barbecue was the easiest option. That way, the men could cook. She liked that idea.

NATALIE AND ADAM ARRIVED FIRST. There were hugs all round. Simon arrived several minutes later. Wendy immediately noticed that his face looked tanned. "Been out in the sun?" she asked as she gave him a hug.

"Yes. I've been surfing." He hugged her back.

"Good for you. With Andy?"

"No, he's been working."

She frowned. "Have you had days off?"

He ran a palm across his face. "I lost my job."

She placed a hand on his shoulder. "Oh, Simon. I'm so sorry. Why didn't you tell me?"

He shrugged as if it didn't matter. "You've had other things on your mind."

"You still could have told me."

"Sorry." His jaw tensed.

She smiled. "It's okay. Come inside." She ushered him in and they began walking towards the kitchen. "How are you coping?"

He sighed heavily. "Not too well. Being let go came as a real shock. I thought I was doing a good job."

Her heart went out to him. He sounded so sad. Defeated. "Let me get you a drink. We should have bought some beers."

"It's okay. Coke's fine."

She lifted a brow. "That's a change."

He shrugged again. "Thought I'd have a few days without alcohol."

"That's not a bad idea." Wendy hesitated, wondering if she should mention the wedding invitation, but she had to, otherwise it would be the elephant in the room. "We got your invitation, Simon."

He turned and found her gaze. "I guess you won't come."

Silence hung in the air. Wendy longed to say more, but she simply replied that they weren't sure. "How would you feel if we don't come?"

He shrugged off-handedly, surprising her. "I won't mind."

"Are you sure?"

"I know you don't agree with marriage between two men."

"No, we don't. But I'd feel bad not being there for you."

His eyes flickered. "*I* might not even go."

Wendy stopped in her tracks and turned to him. "What did you say?"

"I might not even go." His voice was quiet. Barely audible.

"I...I don't understand."

"I'm having second thoughts."

Wendy tried hard to hide her elation. "Really? What's brought that on?"

"My conscience." He held her gaze.

"Oh. I'm sorry." But she wasn't. She was rejoicing inside. "Does Andy know?"

"No. He's been working a lot. We haven't had much time to talk lately."

"I guess he won't be happy."

Simon shook his head. "No, he won't be. He's got it all planned."

She placed her hand on his shoulder. "You're welcome to stay here if you need to."

He smiled. "Thanks. I'll keep that in mind."

"I won't say anything to the others unless you want me to."

"It might be best. Thanks."

"Come on. They'll be waiting for us." She placed her arm around his waist and continued the short distance to the kitchen where the others were standing around chatting.

"Simon. Good to see you." Adam smiled and extended his hand.

Returning his smile, Simon took Adam's hand and shook it. "And you."

Natalie hugged him and Bruce shook his hand. Wendy's heart ached for him. He thought he had everything sorted, but now his life was crashing around him. She gave him an encouraging smile. He could so easily have chosen not to come, but she was thankful he had. It seemed that God was working in his life, and she was excited to see how it would unfold.

"Shall we go outside where it's cooler?" Bruce asked.

"Good idea," Wendy replied. "Hope you brought your swim suits. I forgot to remind you."

"We did," Natalie said.

"So did I," Simon added.

"Good. Let's have a swim before dinner."

They all changed and soon were splashing around in the pool. Wendy sidled up to Bruce. "It's wonderful having them here."

"It is." He pulled her close and planted a kiss on her lips.

"Not in front of the children, darling."

"They're hardly children."

She laughed. "You know what I mean."

"Yes."

"God is good."

"He is."

The evening passed pleasantly. When it came time for them all to leave, Wendy gave Simon a hug and told him she was praying for him. Her heart warmed when he thanked her.

Later, as they prepared for bed, she told Bruce that Simon was reconsidering his relationship with Andy. "I had to tell you, but please don't say anything to anyone. I can't wait to see how this unfolds."

"It sure is an interesting time." He rubbed her arms and looked at her tenderly.

"It is. We just need Elysha to come home now."

"And for you to kiss me."

She laughed. "Do you ever think of anything else?"

"Sometimes." He lowered his lips until they brushed hers.

"Really? Like when?"

He shrugged. "Does it matter?"

"Not really." She responded to his kiss and for a little while forgot about Simon, Natalie, Adam and Elysha. And the fact that Paige had been missing from their family dinner.

CHAPTER 15

*W*hen Simon woke early the following morning, Andy was beside him, snoring loudly. Simon had been in bed when Andy came in late from work the previous evening and had pretended to be asleep. Looking at his partner of three years, and knowing what he was about to do, an ache like he'd never known tore through his heart. Could he really break up with him? They'd enjoyed three wonderful years together. They were lovers, but they were also friends. His throat tightened as he slipped out of bed. Dressing quickly, he scribbled a note and left it on the counter. Memories of their times together flashed through his mind and he almost turned back. But he couldn't deny the call on his life any longer. God had been drawing him to Himself. Gently. Slowly. Convicting of him of his sin. Not just of his homosexuality, but of his broken, rebellious and sinful nature.

He needed one more surfing session with Ellis to get his mind and heart clear. That first afternoon, Ellis hadn't mentioned that he surfed with a number of other men each morning, nor that they shared breakfast afterwards and had a short Bible study and prayer time. This was something Simon discovered when he reached the beach. They were a bunch of misfits. Tom was an alcoholic who'd been sober for two months and was proud of it. Dwayne had recently been released from prison and was trying to get his life in order, and Sam was a drug addict trying to clean his life up. They all had one thing in common—they were all seeking answers for their lives. None of their lifestyle quirks bothered Ellis. He told them God loved them all. It didn't matter about the colour of their skin or what they'd done. They were made in His image, and He had a plan for their lives. God could take their hurts, confusion and rejection and give them new life filled with hope and purpose. No longer did they need to feel like outcasts.

That morning, Simon knew he was on a path that would change his life. The ocean was the most brilliant blue as it shimmered in the early morning sunshine, the white of the waves crashing against the rocks standing out in stark contrast. The grandeur of creation swept over him, and he allowed it to settle into his soul.

He joined the group and paddled with them slowly beyond the breakers. It was so peaceful. If only he could stay there all day and not face Andy. A wave came and he paddled quickly to catch it. The ride was exhilarating. He did it again. And again. And again. Finally, it was time to go in.

The motley group rinsed their salty bodies under the fresh-water showers and then gathered outside Ellis's van for break-fast and a Bible study. Perched on a stool, while the others ate ham and cheese rolls and drank litres of icy cold orange juice, Ellis read a passage from Acts chapter two.

"Therefore, let all Israel be assured of this: God has made this Jesus, whom you crucified, both Lord and Messiah." When the people heard this, they were cut to the heart and said to Peter and the other apostles, "Brothers, what shall we do?" Peter replied, "Repent and be baptized, every one of you, in the name of Jesus Christ for the forgiveness of your sins and you will receive the gift of the Holy Spirit. The promise is for you and your children and for all who are far off—for all whom the Lord our God will call."

Simon's heart quickened. God was speaking to him. *Repent and be baptized.* When Ellis asked if any of them wished to do this, he didn't hesitate. "I do."

The other three also accepted the invitation. They bowed their heads and Ellis led them in a prayer of commitment. He then took them to a quiet rock pool where the water was no deeper than their waists and baptized them in the name of the Father, the Son and the Holy Spirit. It wasn't formal. It wasn't planned. But it was real. As Simon rose from the waters, he truly felt like his old self had gone and had been replaced by a new self. The blood of Jesus Christ had cleansed him of his sin.

Driving home a little later, Simon detoured via the cemetery. Up there, on the cliffs above the ocean, where the wind howled and the seagulls soared, he got down on his knees and wept. Long held grief over losing his father welled inside him. Grief over Paige's untimely death spilled out in wails that racked his body. And then grief over the prospect of losing Andy spilled over in gut wrenching sobs.

Come to me, all you who are weary and burdened, and I will give you rest. Take my yoke upon you and learn from me, for I am gentle and humble in heart, and you will find rest for your souls. For my yoke is easy and my burden is light.

Tears rolled down his cheeks as he leaned against his father's headstone and gazed over the ocean. "Lord, I don't know what the future holds, but I give it to You. Please give rest to my soul and teach me Your ways. I'm so sorry for ignoring You for so long." He turned to his father's grave and inhaled slowly. "Dad, I'm sorry. I know I've disappointed you, but I'll do my best to make it up. I want to make you proud of me." He turned to Paige's grave. "And don't worry, Paige, we'll look after your baby. We'll fight for her to the end if we have to."

His chest felt tight, yet he also felt a freedom of spirit he'd not experienced before. "Lord, I don't know how I'm going to break the news to Andy, but please let him understand. And give me strength to do it." It would be the hardest thing he'd ever done, but it was also the right thing.

Andy was sitting in front of the television eating breakfast when Simon arrived home. He looked up, puzzled, hurt. "You didn't tell me you'd started surfing."

"Sorry. We've been like ships in the night." Simon closed the door, and tossing his wet clothes into the laundry room, sent up a quick prayer.

"I might come with you next time."

Simon tensed, but forced himself to speak calmly. "Great. I'm sure you'll be welcome."

Andy frowned. "Who've you been going with?" A dart of suspicion crossed his face.

"Just some guys."

"Gays?"

"No." Simon opened the fridge and pulled out a Coke. "Want one?"

"Already got one." Andy held the can up.

Simon pulled the ringtop and took a long slug. The fizz got to him and he belched. "Sorry."

"Is something wrong. You seem on edge."

"Do I?"

"Yes." Andy looked at him, his brows knitted.

Simon reached for courage. The moment had come—he could no longer avoid it. "I've got something to tell you."

Andy's head tilted. "Are you sick?"

"No. Nothing like that."

"What is it, then?"

Simon bolstered his courage and moved to the table. Andy remained on the couch but his gaze was fixed on Simon's. Simon pulled out a chair and sat. "I can't marry you, Andy. I'm sorry." He gulped.

Andy's face darkened. His muscles tensed and bulged under his T-shirt. "Don't do this, Simon. Everything's booked."

"I know. I'm sorry." Simon thought it interesting that Andy hadn't replied by saying he loved and needed him. For the first time, Simon got a glimpse into Andy's true character. It wasn't so much about their relationship, it seemed. It was about the wedding. About being different. About going against mainstream beliefs. How had he missed that?

"Why?" A muscle quivered in Andy's jaw.

"I gave my heart to the Lord this morning." Strength surged through Simon as he held Andy's shocked gaze.

Andy's eyes narrowed. "I knew you were going soft. I knew it. So, this is the end?"

"Yes. I'm sorry."

"Go." He waved his arm angrily. "Before I do something I'll regret."

Despite Andy's reaction, which Simon believed was a knee-jerk response, a flicker of compassion swept through him. "I'd still like to be friends. It doesn't have to end this way."

"I don't know how you can say that! I don't ever want to see you again."

Simon shook his head as sadness and regret flowed through him. He realised then that his hands were trembling. Andy might not be the man he'd portrayed himself to be, but they'd been close for three years. To have it end this way was heart wrenching. He stood and grabbed a bag from the hall cupboard. He couldn't take everything now, he'd have to come back. Where would he go? Mum's? The church? He packed the essential shirts and shorts, socks and jocks, along with the photo of him and Paige Mum had given him for Christmas, and the Bible she'd given him when he was ten which he'd found when he unpacked the boxes he'd shifted from her house recently.

Andy remained on the couch, his gaze fixed on the television. Other than tensing, he didn't move when Simon said good-bye.

"I'll come back later for the rest."

Andy ignored him.

Placing his hand on the door handle, Simon paused. He was tempted to look back, but then remembered the verse where Jesus said that *'No one, after putting his hand to the plow and looking back, is fit for the kingdom of God.'* No, he wouldn't look back. He'd only remember what God had saved him from. He wouldn't look back with longing at a lifestyle that had led him astray.

As he opened the door, Andy spoke quietly. "You might want to get yourself tested for HIV."

Simon stopped, frozen, unable to move. He turned around slowly and walked towards Andy. "What are you saying?"

Andy looked up and shrugged. "Work it out."

"No, you tell me. Do you have it?"

The resigned expression in Andy's eyes was all the answer Simon needed. He sat beside Andy. "Why didn't you tell me?"

"I didn't want you to stay because I have the virus."

Simon's mind whirled. As far as he knew, neither he nor Andy had had any other partners since becoming a couple. But if Andy had been recently diagnosed, it meant he'd been unfaithful. But did it matter? Sin was sin. He felt betrayed, but he also was thankful that he now knew the unconditional, unchanging love of God that had cleansed him of his sin and offered him hope and a future. "I'm so sorry. How long have you known?"

"A few weeks."

"And you didn't think to tell me?"

"I didn't know how."

"Is that why you were so eager to get married quickly?"

"Partly. I wanted you to know how sorry I was, but also how much I love you."

It was too late. Would it have made a difference if Andy had told him earlier? Simon somehow doubted it. God had been tapping him on the shoulder for some time. "You should have told me. Are you on medication?"

Andy nodded.

"Is your job safe?"

"Yes. They know, and they've been fine about it."

Simon drew a breath. "I guess getting the disease was always a risk."

"Yes." Tears filled Andy's eyes. "I've let you down. It was so stupid. Is…is there any way you'll reconsider staying?" His eyes pleaded with Simon's.

The swell of pain in Simon's chest was beyond tears. "I'm so sorry. I truly did give my heart to the Lord this morning. I can't do this anymore, but I'd like to remain friends."

Andy managed a sad smile. "I'd like that."

Simon returned his smile. "Good. That makes me feel better. I'll still go, but I'll be back for the rest of my things."

"Come back whenever you want. And make sure you get tested."

"I will."

Andy dipped his head. "Give me a hug?"

Unable to deny him, Simon shuffled along the couch and drew Andy close. His body shook as he sobbed against Simon's shoulder. Simon felt wretched leaving him like this, but he couldn't continue the relationship now that He'd committed himself to God. "I love you, Andy. God bless you."

Releasing himself from Andy's arms, he stood and headed for the door. This time, after picking up his bag, he looked back and gave a small wave before stepping out the door.

CHAPTER 16

*C*olin paced the floor of his living room. Annie's ultimatum weighed heavily on him, but she hadn't budged an inch. There had to be some way of convincing her, because he didn't want to have to choose between her and Elysha.

When Paige's brother, Simon, had gone into the bar looking for him, Annie told him and he went out and tracked Simon down. He'd never expected to be knocked out by him. If he had to, he'd use that in his case to get Elysha. Surely the court would think twice about giving a baby to a family whose members went around beating innocent people.

Using the underground Goth network, he'd heard that there was a weakness in the Department of Child Service's computer systems and one of his fellow Goths had discovered where Elysha was and told him. It would be risky going there, but if only Annie could see her, he was sure she'd change her mind. Time was running out. He had no choice.

He poked his head into the back room where Annie was painting. An excellent artist, her dark paintings brought in more money than their bartending incomes combined. "Annie, let's go out for a while."

She looked up. "Do we have to? I'm right in the middle of this."

"Yes, we do. And wear regular clothes."

She narrowed her eyes. They rarely wore clothes with any colour, choosing instead to wear all black. "All right. Give me a few minutes."

"Okay." He returned to pacing. The next question was how to see the baby. Knock on the door? Pretend to be someone from Child Services? Peer through a window? Wait until someone took her outside? He pulled at his hair. Useless. It was all useless. They'd get caught and that would be it. He slumped onto the couch. Maybe he should just give up.

He was still slumped when Annie emerged a few minutes later. She'd done what he'd asked and was wearing a short summer shift and sandals. Her legs were long and pale, not surprising since they never saw the sun. "I thought we were going out."

He sighed. "I've changed my mind."

She frowned and sat beside him. "What's wrong?"

"I'm trying to think of ways to get you to change your mind."

"About the baby? I thought you'd decided not to go to court tomorrow."

He shrugged. "I lied."

She met his gaze without flinching. "I don't understand why you want her so much."

"Because she's mine. I'm her father." He poked his chest with his own finger and straightened. He could feel the anger and frustration growing inside him.

"You know nothing about being a father."

"Does anyone at the beginning?"

"Maybe not. But you've had no role model, no family to speak of, no siblings. How do expect to raise a child?"

"With your help."

She sank into the seat beside him and sighed. "I'm not ready to be a mother. I'm really sorry, but if I was going to care for a baby, it'd be my own, not someone else's."

"But she's *my* baby. Paige might have been her mother, but she's also mine."

"Well, good luck with that."

"Can't we work something out? What if I ask for joint custody? Or even an occasional visit?" He was clutching at straws.

She huffed with exasperation. "Whatever."

"Do you mean that? Really?"

"You're not going to give in, I can see that."

He sat straighter and took her hand. "I don't want to give in. I never had parents who loved me. I don't want my baby to grow up not knowing me."

"I guess we could learn." She sounded defeated.

His heart swelled. "Those are the sweetest words I've heard all day."

"What do I have to do if I come with you?"

"I'm not sure, but be prepared to convince them you'll be a good mother to Elysha."

She raised a brow. "Like that will be easy."

"Just do your best, Annie. I'm sure you'll charm them."

"I'm glad you have confidence. I truly have no idea what end's what on a baby."

"We could do some studying."

She let out an irritated sigh. "Okay. Whatever."

Excited, Colin opened his laptop and typed in the search bar, *'how to care for a baby'.* Almost five billion results came up. He gulped.

"I need a drink," Annie said, standing. "Want one?"

"Yes, please." His gaze didn't waver from the first entry. *A newborn baby needs to be fed every 2 to 3 hours...*

NATALIE CHECKED her notes for the hundredth time. She wouldn't be caught unawares about anything. She and Adam were teachers and had plenty of experience with older children, but they'd never had a baby. Since the day they'd discovered that Colin Daley was contesting custody, they'd studied everything they could put their hands on. There was very little they didn't know about caring for a newborn.

If the decision was based on financial security, they'd win hands down. Colin Daley hadn't even had enough money for the DNA test at the beginning. They owned their own home. They both had secure jobs, and in fact, Adam was studying for his Master's in Education with a view to becoming a school principal. She would stop work if they were granted custody of Elysha. She didn't need to work. They'd also win hands down on lifestyle and beliefs. They were good, upright Christians, involved in both their church and wider community. Colin

Daley was a Goth. They'd heard he had a partner but knew little about her. But they guessed it wouldn't come down to that. He was Elysha's father. Natalie was Elysha's aunt.

She reminded herself that they had God on their side, although several times, despite herself, Natalie had stopped and questioned if it was better for Elysha to be with her father, or with them. They could give her more opportunities in life, and they'd love her to bits, but would Elysha miss her birth parents if she didn't have the opportunity to know either of them? Was Natalie being selfish because she and Adam couldn't have children of their own?

She experienced a gamut of perplexing emotions. If they weren't awarded care of Elysha, she would be utterly distraught, but guilt would also weigh on her if they did. She had no choice but to leave the decision with God and trust Him with the outcome.

CHAPTER 17

*R*ising early on the day of the court hearing, Wendy spent longer than normal with her devotions while Bruce was out riding. Like her, she knew he'd also be seeking the Lord's blessing over the court proceedings while riding Prince.

Finishing her devotions, she set her Bible on the coffee table and gazed out the window, her thoughts and prayers very much on Natalie, Adam and Elysha. She prayed fervently that the court would grant Natalie and Adam custody of Elysha, and yet, her Bible reading had once again reinforced the importance of trusting God, regardless. He was sovereign, and His ways were best, but her stomach still churned as she awaited the outcome.

Pushing to her feet, she caught a glimpse of Bruce entering the top paddock astride Prince. He looked so dashing that her heart did a flip. She still had to pinch herself to make sure she wasn't dreaming that he was her husband. God had blessed her so much by bringing him into her life, and she didn't know how she would have survived the past few months if he hadn't been by her side.

She walked to the kitchen and turned the coffee machine on. No doubt he'd be ready for a cup when he came in. She busied herself preparing their breakfast and had it ready by the time she heard boots scraping on the steps.

"Coffee smells mighty good," he called from the back porch.

She poked her head around the corner. He was sitting on the steps pulling his boots off, and the heady scent of his after-shave wafted in the air and made her heart flutter. "Did you have a good ride, darling?" she asked softly.

"Yes. You should come with me one morning." He looked up at her and winked.

Shaking her head, she let out a small chuckle. "You're not giving up, are you?"

"Nope. Not until you decide to come again."

She threw her head back and laughed. "What hope have I got?"

"Not much." Standing, he closed the gap between them and rubbed her arms while gazing into her eyes. "I know you'd enjoy it, and I'd enjoy having you with me."

She blew out a breath. "I'll give it some thought." She had to face her fears, she knew that. And if she were honest, the thought of riding with Bruce did hold appeal.

"Good. I'll have Marcy ready tomorrow morning."

Her eyes enlarged. "I didn't say I'd go tomorrow."

He stole a kiss and winked. "No time like the present."

She lifted her hand to his cheek. "Let's see what happens today," she said quietly.

He grimaced. "You're right. That was thoughtless of me."

"No problem." She took his hand. "Come and have breakfast, and then we need to get ready."

AN HOUR LATER, dressed in her best skirt, pale blue cashmere top, and the pearls Bruce had given her as a wedding gift, Wendy slid into the car beside him. She grinned at his appearance. Dark trousers and dress shoes instead of jeans and boots. He looked very smart indeed.

They'd agreed to meet Natalie and Adam outside the courthouse at ten a.m. The hearing was scheduled for half an hour later. Wendy had tried calling Simon several times to give him the details but had only reached his voicemail. She wondered if he'd talked with Andy yet, and continued to send up prayers for him. She also wondered if he'd turn up today. She prayed he would.

Bruce parked the car, paid for three hours at the meter although they had no idea how long they'd need, and then took Wendy's hand as they walked towards the solid stone heritage-listed building. Although it was still early in the day, the sun warmed her back and soothed her spirit.

Natalie and Adam were already there, standing hand-in-hand near the entrance. Natalie was wearing a simple, but elegant cream linen dress that enhanced her slim figure. Two-inch heels brought her face to face with Adam, who looked business-like in his dark suit. If appearances could influence the court's decision, Wendy felt they would have the edge.

After hugs and kisses all round, Adam suggested they have

coffee at the café attached to the courthouse and they all agreed.

"Is Simon coming?" Natalie asked Wendy as they followed the men.

"I've tried calling him but he hasn't answered. I hope he comes," Wendy replied.

"He seemed different the other night."

Wendy bit her lip. Should she say something or leave it to him to tell them he was thinking of cancelling the wedding? She decided to say nothing in case he'd changed his mind, although she prayed he hadn't. If his relationship with Andy had ended, he might not be in good shape, especially since he'd also lost his job. She'd look for him afterwards if he didn't turn up. She gave Natalie a tentative smile. "He did seem a little different, didn't he?"

Nodding, Natalie adjusted her handbag straps and then turned to look at Wendy. "Adam and I have decided to go to the wedding, even though we don't agree with it. Simon's family, after all."

Wendy drew a long breath. It was becoming harder not to say anything. "I'm sure he'll be happy about that. Bruce and I are still undecided." That was the truth. The wedding hadn't officially been cancelled, and she and Bruce hadn't decided one way or the other.

The men ordered the coffee and chose a table in the outside area, bordered on three sides with tubs overflowing with colourful annuals. Wendy saw Simon first. She broke into a wide smile and waved. He lifted his hand in acknowledgment and headed their way. She was pleased that he'd also chosen to dress well for the occasion. He looked smart in tailored, dark trousers, a button-down shirt and a conservative red tie. Tears sprang to her eyes. He looked so handsome...would he ever find true love? Her heart ached for him and she sent up another prayer.

She held out her hand as he reached the table. "I'm so glad you made it, Simon."

He bent down and kissed her on the cheek. "Sorry I didn't answer your calls."

She met his gaze and raised her brows at him without making it obvious to the others.

His slight nod and wistful expression told her all she needed to know.

She patted his hand. "No problem. You're here now. Would you like a coffee?"

"Yes, but I can get it."

She held him back. "Bruce can order it. It's okay."

He gave her an appreciative smile. "Thanks." He greeted the others and then sat.

Nobody seemed to know what to say. It had all been said before. It was a matter of waiting, and time was passing so slowly.

"How are you feeling?" Simon eventually asked Natalie.

She shrugged. Tucked some hair behind her ear. "Oh, you know, wishing it was all over."

"Waiting must be horrible."

She nodded, her eyes filling.

Simon handed her a tissue. "Sorry."

She thanked him and dabbed her eyes carefully. Their coffees arrived and they all thanked the waitress and then began sipping.

Beside her, Simon tensed. Wendy followed his gaze. She guessed that the tall, thin man with long, dark hair tied in a ponytail was Colin Daley. Dressed in tan chinos and a white button-down shirt, he seemed quite presentable. Not at all how Paige had described him. As Wendy studied him, the realisation that he was Elysha's father fully dawned on her, and once again, she was surprised that she felt compassion, not animosity, towards him. *Could God work this out so there were no losers?*

The others turned their heads, following the direction of hers and Simon's gazes. "That's him," Simon said. Beside him, an equally tall, dark-haired young woman gripped his hand as they walked tentatively towards the entrance of the courthouse. Wearing a short dress, her legs were as pale as a lily. Wendy guessed they rarely saw the light of day. Paige had grown pale like that in the years she'd been a Goth, her face so translucent it looked like porcelain. This must be the girl who'd replaced her as Colin's girlfriend. Wendy was unsure how she felt about them, but the words of Jesus came back to her:

"If you love those who love you, what credit is that to you? Even sinners love those who love them. And if you do good to those who are good to you, what credit is that to you? Even sinners do that... "*You have heard that it was said, 'Love your neighbor and hate your enemy.' But I tell you, love your enemies and pray for those who persecute you, that you may be children of your Father in heaven. He causes His sun to rise on the evil and the good, and sends rain on the righteous and the unrighteous. If you love those who love you, what reward will you get? Are not even the tax collectors doing that? And if you greet only your own people, what are you doing more than*

others? Do not even pagans do that? Be perfect, therefore, as your heavenly Father is perfect."

It was a tall order, but as challenging as it might be, to be true to their faith and to God, that's what they had to do. Be kind and merciful and love their enemies. Bruce squeezed her hand and she guessed he was having similar thoughts. Elysha's future lay in the balance, but most importantly, the family needed to be found worthy of their calling as followers of Jesus.

"I think it's time to go in. Miranda will be waiting for us," Adam said. "Shall we pray before we go?"

Everyone nodded and bowed their heads, even Simon, which Wendy found curious.

"Dear Heavenly Father," Adam's voice was clear and steady, "we once again bring Elysha's future before You. Lord, we ask that Your will, not ours, be done, although You know that the desire of our hearts is for her to come home with Natalie and me. Whatever happens, help us to bring glory and honour to You in our actions, thoughts and deeds. Be with the magistrate now as we go before him or her. In Jesus' precious name. Amen."

A round of quiet 'Amens' followed before they rose and entered the courthouse.

CHAPTER 18

$\mathcal{T}$he court room was smaller than Wendy had expected. No larger than their living room, a long desk stretched along the front with three rows of chairs facing it. Other than Colin Daley, his partner, Natalie and Adam's legal representative, Miranda Murphy, and two official looking women Wendy didn't know but guessed were from Child Services, the room was empty, cold and quiet. She followed Bruce to take a seat in the second row. Simon sat on her other side. Natalie and Adam joined Miranda in the front row and spoke with her in hushed tones.

Bruce squeezed Wendy's hand. Her stomach was filled with butterflies despite her resolve to leave the outcome with God. It was such a momentous and life-changing occasion for everyone. She turned and gave him a small smile. Her gaze then shifted to Colin Daley and his partner who appeared to be representing themselves. She guessed they couldn't afford a lawyer.

At exactly half past ten, a door at the front opened and the presiding magistrate, a woman Wendy guessed was in her late fifties, swept into the room. Everyone stood while she walked behind the desk, pulled out the large wing-backed chair, and sat.

Spreading her sheaf of papers in front of her, she peered over her glasses, leaned forward and briefly addressed the official women. She then straightened and introduced herself to everyone else as Justice Jennifer Bowman.

"I'm presiding over this hearing today between..." Pausing, she adjusted her glasses and picked up one of the papers, studying it before continuing. "Colin Daley, the applicant, and Adam and Natalie Jenkins, the respondents, concerning the custody of Elysha Grace Miller." She then asked the applicant and respondents to stand and identify themselves, which they did.

"I believe that Mr. Daley is the father of the child in question. Is that correct?" She peered over her glasses again at the women, who stated it was. "He's also representing himself?"

"Yes," the younger of the two replied.

"The mother is deceased?" Once again, the women concurred. The magistrate picked up another of the papers and studied it before addressing Colin. "Why would I consider granting custody of this child to you, Mr. Daley? It appears that the mother, Paige Elysha Miller, was either unaware of whom the father of her child was or that she chose to withhold that information for a reason. Can you give me any good reasons why I should consider your application?"

Wendy clutched Bruce's hand as Colin Daley stood, twisting his hands together in front of him. "Well, Your

Honour," he cleared his throat, "I might not have any experience with children, but I believe that all children deserve to be raised by at least one of their parents. She's my daughter, and I'd love the opportunity to raise her." He briefly glanced down at his partner. She squeezed his hand and gave him a small smile that appeared forced. "Annie and I will learn. We want to give Elysha the best life possible. We might not have much, but we'll give her love."

Justice Bowman studied him for a few moments. "Do you have any family support?"

Colin's face was already pale, but Wendy was convinced it paled even further. "We don't. That's one of the reasons I want her so much. You see, my mother died in childbirth, just like Paige did. I never knew her, and I didn't know my father, either. I was raised in the foster care system. I don't want that to happen to Elysha."

"You were never adopted?"

"No." His Adam's apple bobbed in his throat when he gulped.

The magistrate scribbled some notes and then looked up again. "So, you have no one who can offer support? Not even your partner's family?"

"No, Annie's from Sweden. Her family's there."

"And she has permanent residency status?"

Colin visibly tensed, as did Annie. Wendy wondered if she was in the country illegally. "Y…yes." He gulped again.

"That's all, Mr. Daley. You may sit." She then turned her attention to Miranda Murphy. "You're representing the respondents, Ms. Murphy?"

"I am, Your Honour."

"Tell me why I should consider granting custody to them. I believe that the woman, Mrs. Jenkins, is the baby's aunt?"

"Yes, Your Honour." She proceeded to tell Justice Bowman what wonderful, upright citizens Natalie and Adam were, and what loving parents they would be to baby Elysha. "They've already bonded with her, Your Honour, having been with her since birth. They've also lodged a formal adoption application which has unfortunately been suspended until this matter is resolved."

"And they don't have other children?"

"No, Your Honour. However, they're both teachers and have had plenty of experience with children."

Justice Bowman removed her glasses and placed them on the desk. Her focus shifted to the two women. "Does the department have any recommendations or further information I should be aware of before I make my decision?"

The older woman stood and removed her pink-rimmed glasses. "We do, Your Honour. The department has found no reason not to award custody to the father. He has a clean record, he's employed, and has been residing in the same apartment for a number of years. We consider him to be safe, Your Honour."

Wendy's throat went dry. In front of her, Natalie let out a small whimper.

"I see. Thank you, Ms. Scott." Justice Bowman remained silent for several moments. She drummed her fingers on the desk. Other than that, the silence was palpable and Wendy expected that Bruce could hear her heart thumping. "Will both the applicant and the respondents please stand?"

They did. Wendy clutched Bruce's arm.

"This is not an easy matter to rule on. There are reasons for me to consider granting custody to both parties, however, I cannot see any solid reason to deny the child the opportunity to live with her biological father."

Natalie gasped and reached for Adam. Retaining his upright stance, he slipped his arm around her shoulder and pulled her tight.

The magistrate held up her hand. "However, I also believe the child has the right to know her mother's family. While I'm granting custody to the applicant, I also stipulate that the respondents and their family be given reasonable access to the child. I'm hesitant at this stage to rule on how many hours per week is reasonable, as I hope you can sort all that out amicably. Mr. Daley, you would do well to befriend the child's maternal family since you've stated you have none of your own. They may well become the family you've never had and may be able to offer you and your partner the support you need to raise this child properly."

She turned her gaze to Natalie and Adam, her voice softening. "I hope you can find it within yourselves to work together with the applicant for the good of the child. I know this isn't what you wanted, but we must keep in mind that this is about what's best for the child, and no reason has been presented to me that suggests she shouldn't be with her father. I'm sorry."

"Yes, Your Honour. We'll do our best," Adam replied. He tried to sound confident, but the wobble in his voice betrayed him.

Although her heart was breaking, Wendy was proud of him. Wasn't this exactly what God had imprinted on her heart less than an hour before? He must have been preparing them all for this outcome. They had to work together for Elysha's good, overcome their prejudices and angst, and learn to co-operate. She prayed they'd all be mature enough to do just that. But more importantly, she prayed that baby Elysha would be loved and cared for.

The final moments of the hearing were taken up with formalities. Colin and Annie were to collect baby Elysha from the department's offices that afternoon. Justice Bowman wished them all the best and gave them a final word of advice. "Don't be too proud to ask for help. I don't want baby Elysha to become a statistic."

"Thank you, Your Honour. We won't, and she won't. You can be sure of that." Colin's elation was in stark contrast to Natalie's obvious despair.

"I'm glad to hear that." The magistrate rose, nodded, and exited through the same door she'd entered by.

Wendy closed her eyes briefly and prayed for Natalie. This would be so hard on her. She'd be devastated. *Lord, please help us, especially Natalie, to get through this. It's not what we wanted, but Lord, we'd trusted You with the outcome, and this is it. Please help us to reach out to Colin and Annie and befriend them, and please help them to allow us to do that.*

She brushed her tears from her cheeks and then stood resolutely. Her daughter needed her.

COLIN COULDN'T BELIEVE IT. Elysha was theirs! He swept Annie off her feet and twirled her around. "Can you believe it, Annie? We're parents!"

She let out a nervous laugh. "I can't…"

"It's going to be wonderful! We have a baby!" He set her back on the floor and hugged and kissed her.

"Colin. Calm down. Everybody's watching."

"Does it matter?"

"Yes." She nodded to the side. "They're waiting to talk with us."

His gaze followed the direction of her nod. Paige's sister and her husband stood watching them. He held her hand tightly. Colin turned back to face Annie. "We don't need them, Annie. We'll figure it out on our own."

"But the judge…"

"Don't worry about what she said. Nobody will check." He smiled at her, willing her to share his enthusiasm.

She gave him a droll look. "I hope you know what you're doing."

"Of course I do. I read about looking after babies last night. It's going to be a piece of cake."

"Whatever."

Colin turned his head when Paige's sister and her husband stepped towards them. The husband cleared his throat.

"Mr. Daley. Colin. Can we call you that?"

"Sure. And you are?" Colin knew full well who he was, but hey, make the guy sweat a little more.

"Adam. And this is Natalie." He placed his arm gently around her shoulders. Her eyes were red and puffy and grew moist when he hugged her. "We're hoping we can arrange a time to see Elysha. We won't make a fuss, but we miss her terribly."

Colin shrugged. "Give us a week to get her settled in and then we'll see."

"We won't cause trouble, but we'd love to see her before then if possible," Adam pleaded.

"Give me your number. I'll call you."

Adam reached into his back pocket and took out his wallet. Pulling out a business card, he scribbled his name and number on the back and handed it to him.

Colin took the card and placed it in his pocket.

"May we have yours?"

Colin pursed his lips. They weren't going to give up.

Annie grabbed his arm. "Give it to them, Colin."

He huffed in exasperation but finally agreed. He scribbled his name and number on a piece of paper and handed it to Adam.

"Thank you. And all the best with Elysha. Give her a kiss from us." Adam's voice faltered.

How did he answer that? He shrugged. "Yeah, okay."

Adam held out his hand and Colin had no choice but to shake it. As he did, he caught sight of Simon standing behind Adam with his arms crossed, glaring at him. What gall! He had a good mind to walk over and punch the guy, get him back for beating him up the other day, only this wasn't the place. Instead, he held his gaze long enough for him to know he should watch his back.

He grabbed Annie's hand. "Come on, Annie, let's get out of here."

endy and Bruce, along with Simon, returned with Natalie and Adam to their home. Although they'd given lip service to accepting that the court might grant custody to Colin Daley, they'd never truly believed it would happen. But it had, and the mood in the room was sombre. How did one face such great disappointment?

Wendy recalled the sermon that John Hodges, the pastor at their new church, had given recently about why God doesn't always answer prayers the way we want Him to.

God is good and knows what's eternally best for us. He sometimes says 'no' because He has something better in store. Something we haven't even thought to ask for. Ephesians 3:20 says that 'He can do immeasurably more than all we can ask or imagine.' Trust His timing. Trust His 'no'. And trust His idea of what's best for you, eternally. He truly is a good Father. His ways are higher than ours and He knows what's best for us.

But it was almost impossible to think of anything He might have in store that could be better. Wendy was positive this wasn't what Paige would have wanted for Elysha, and although the magistrate had instructed Colin Daley and his partner to befriend their family and allow them access to her, he'd been less than eager to even give Adam his number. Wendy sensed it might take another trip to court for them to even see her.

It was hard to maintain trust when the wind had been taken out of their sails well and truly. But this was the time when their focus needed to be on God and what He wanted, not on their disappointment, otherwise their faith meant nothing.

"Can I get anyone anything?" Adam asked after they'd all gathered in the living room.

Wendy shook her head. "No thanks, Adam. I'm fine for now." The others concurred, even though it was past lunchtime.

Adam sat beside Natalie and took her hand. She'd barely said a word since the magistrate announced her decision. Wendy's heart squeezed with pain for her daughter. She leaned forward and spoke quietly. "The only thing we can do is pray. Our trust is in God, and we must entrust Elysha to Him as well. I'm happy to start."

No one argued. They bowed their heads.

Wendy took a slow breath. "Lord God, we come before You with sad hearts. We'd all hoped that baby Elysha would be coming home today, but that wasn't to be. We entrust her to Your care, and we ask that You'll watch over her new parents. Give them wisdom, and may they give her all the love she needs and deserves. And Lord God, I pray for Natalie and

Adam. Comfort them in their time of grief and disappointment. May they know the peace that passeth all understanding as they face this new reality. In Your precious Son's name. Amen."

One by one, the others prayed until Simon was left. Wendy knew she wasn't the only one surprised to hear him clear his throat after Natalie finished her brief, heart-felt prayer. Tears of gratitude stung her eyes as he began to pray. "God, I'm not very good at this, but I hope You'll hear me. I'm sorry for hitting Colin the other day. I don't know if that made a difference to the outcome, but if it did, I'll do anything to make it right. I think the judge made the wrong decision. They shouldn't have been given Elysha. Please let them return her to Natalie and Adam. They're her parents. That's all for now. In Jesus' name. Amen."

A round of quiet 'Amen's' followed. When they raised their heads, Wendy caught Simon's gaze and raised a brow.

He nodded and took a breath. "I've got some news." All eyes turned to him. Natalie glanced at Wendy and frowned. Wendy gave a small smile and returned her gaze to Simon. She was so proud of him.

He blew out his breath. "I'm not sure where to start."

Wendy reached out and patted his leg. "You'll be fine. Start anywhere."

"Okay." He looked down and stared at his fingernails. "I've broken up with Andy. There's not going to be a wedding."

Natalie and Adam gasped, their eyes widening.

"But that's not all." He raised his head. "I've recommitted my life to the Lord as well."

All their eyes widened further, including Wendy's. This was

more than she expected but it was the answer to the prayer she'd been praying for so long. That Simon would return to the faith of his childhood. That he'd find peace in God, forgiveness for his sins, and new life in Jesus.

"I knew something was different," Natalie said. "That's wonderful news." She threw her arms around him. "I'm so happy for you."

Simon smiled. "Thank you."

"How is Andy handling the break up?" she asked.

Simon's lips twisted. "Not too well. He's got HIV."

"Oh dear. You didn't tell me that," Wendy said, her mind whirling. "Does…does…?"

"Does that mean I have it?"

She nodded.

"I have to be tested. It's possible. But it's okay. There's medication. I'll be all right, and I might not have it."

"Let's pray that you don't." Wendy rubbed his arm and sent up a silent prayer.

"Well, that sure is a lot of news to take in." Standing, Bruce rubbed his hands together. "I'm going to make a cup of tea. Would anyone like one now?"

This time, they all said they would, and little by little, the shock subsided and they began to talk and plan.

"We'll give him a few days and then we'll call him," Adam said as he sipped his tea.

"I think that's long enough," Wendy agreed.

"And if we need to go back to court, we will," Natalie said with resolve.

"I don't think it'll come to that," Simon said. "I'd give him and his partner a week with the baby at the most. They won't last any longer than that."

"How do you know that? He looked stoked," Natalie retorted.

Simon shrugged. "Just a hunch."

"Don't do anything stupid, Simon." Natalie frowned. "Did you really punch him?"

He grimaced and then nodded. "Yep. Not proud of it. It definitely wasn't my finest moment. But that's when I met Ellis and my life changed."

Natalie frowned. "Ellis? He's not gay too, is he?"

"No." Simon shook his head and chuckled. "He's the guy I've been surfing with. He's a counsellor at The Emmaus Chapel."

"Oh. Well, that's good. We'll have to meet him sometime."

"Yeah. He's a cool dude."

Wendy squeezed Bruce's hand. When he turned his head and looked at her and their gazes connected, she gave him a small nod. It was time to go. He got the message.

"I think we'll head off, if that's okay. Let us know if we can do anything at all, and we'll be sure to keep praying," he said.

"That's fine." Adam stood and shook his hand. "Thanks for your support. We truly appreciate it."

Bruce patted him on the shoulder. "We're just so sorry it didn't work out the way we wanted."

"It certainly didn't."

After bidding them all goodbye, Wendy and Bruce got into their car and headed back to the farm. Although her heart was still heavy, a sense of peace and calm had settled inside her. She turned her head and looked at Bruce. "I have a feeling that somehow this is going to work out. I don't know how, but God has impressed on me to trust Him. To abide in Him. I feel like Job. Well, not quite, but with Paige, and now Elysha, it's like we're being tested."

"Our faith is definitely being tested, that's for sure. But God is good. We must never forget that. And yes, I somehow think it's going to work out, too."

She sat quietly for a few moments, twiddling her rings. "I was thinking I might like to go for a ride this afternoon."

His mouth tipped in a pleased grin. "Wonderful! I'll saddle Marcy as soon as we get home."

"I still don't have any jeans."

He chuckled. "They're not a requirement, love, but we could stop on our way home, get some late lunch, and buy a pair."

"Sounds good. Let's do it." Although going straight home held more appeal, returning to everyday life was a stepping stone to coping with her grief. Wendy never thought she'd wear a pair of jeans, but maybe it was time to step outside her comfort zone and do things that stretched her.

"I don't think they're very flattering," she said to Bruce later after putting them on at home.

Stepping towards her, he placed his hands gently on her upper arms and gazed into her eyes. "I think you're beautiful regardless of what you're wearing. Or not wearing." His eyes twinkled with mischief.

"Bruce!" She slapped him lightly and laughed, but when he lowered his face and his lips touched hers, she melted into his arms and lost herself in his kiss.

Reluctantly, she pulled away. "We'll never go riding if we don't stop this."

He looked disappointed but agreed. "Come on then, let's saddle the horses and get going. We can finish this later."

Her heart warmed when he stole another quick kiss. God had truly known what He was doing when He brought Bruce into her life. Having him beside her, loving her and caring for her, made such a difference, and she knew beyond a shadow of a doubt that they'd get through this time of grief and sadness and learn to enjoy life again. One day at a time. One step at a time. One moment at a time.

LATER, sitting atop Marcy, the old mare Bruce had selected for her because of her staid nature, Wendy wondered why she'd made so much fuss about not going riding. Clip-clopping beside Bruce, who was riding the much larger Prince, along the quiet trails near their farm was peaceful and revitalising. She chose not to chastise herself for not taking her phone with her on that fateful day. Paige had died, and there was no way of reversing it. There was no way of knowing if it would have made a difference had she had her phone with her. Accepting what had happened was part of dealing with her grief.

"We should do this more often," she said as they reached a row of large, shady poinciana trees covered in bright orange flowers.

"That would be wonderful, darlin'." Reaching over, he squeezed her hand and winked. "And I love seeing you in jeans."

She shook her head and chuckled. "Don't tell the children."

"You'll have to pay me a lot of money not to."

"You're incorrigible, Bruce McCarthy!"

"I love it when you're fired up." He threw his head back and laughed.

CHAPTER 20

*H*aving studied on the Internet what baby items they'd need if they were awarded Elysha, Colin dragged Annie into the local charity stores looking for a pram and a cot. They also needed clothes, baby formula and bottles, as well as sterilising equipment and nappies. They had less than two hours to collect it all.

"I hope you know what you're doing," Annie said as she followed him along a row of used baby goods.

"I do," he said, stopping to inspect yet another pram. "This one looks good. I think we'll get it."

She shrugged off-handedly. "Whatever. It's your money."

He glared at her before quickly changing his tune. "It's going to be great, Annie. Wait until you see her."

"I can't wait," she replied, her tone droll.

He carried on regardless. She'd fall in love with Elysha as soon as they met. He glanced at the clock on the wall. They were running out of time. "Come on, let's pay for this. We can get the rest later."

"We'll need nappies and formula before picking her up. I know that much."

He scratched his head. "You're right. We'll stop at the pharmacy on our way."

More than an hour and two buses later, they arrived at the Child Services main building, ten minutes late. Annie raised her brow. "Not so easy, hey?"

The first hurdle had been trying to collapse the pram. It was more complicated than Colin had expected, so he left it up. The second hurdle was getting it on and off the buses without bumping into people. At least they'd been able to practice without Elysha. They'd do better on the return journey. "It's okay. Come on, let's go meet her." He hurried ahead, pushing the pram towards the main entrance. His heart pounded. This was the moment he'd been waiting for.

The double doors opened automatically. He approached the reception desk on the left and a middle-aged woman wearing a blue uniform looked up. "Can I help you?"

"Colin Daley to collect Elysha Daley. Sorry. Elysha Miller." He gulped. They'd need to get her name changed officially.

The woman returned her gaze to the computer screen and studied it with a narrow gaze. Colin grew alarmed. Was there a problem? Finally, she raised her head. "Take a seat and I'll call the case worker." She nodded towards the waiting area filled with chairs and people. There was hardly a vacant chair. A TV sat on the wall playing the news.

"Thank you." He gave her a nod and shuffled into the waiting area. A woman with two small children playing on the floor moved some toys off the seat beside her. "You can sit here."

He smiled. "Thank you." There was only one chair. "Take it, Annie. I can stand."

She shot him a look of exasperation. She didn't want to be here. He knew that. But she sat, and he gave her an encouraging smile as he leaned against the wall. The woman started chatting with her. He grew anxious when one of the children, a little girl wearing a cute red dress and white sandals, bumped Annie's legs and held up a doll.

He relaxed when Annie smiled at the girl and took the doll. There was hope. *Or was she simply acting?*

Fifteen minutes later, Ms. Scott, the older woman from the court hearing that morning, called his name. He motioned for Annie to follow him. She stood and said goodbye to the little girl and her mother.

Colin grabbed her hand with one of his and pushed the pram with the other as they hurried along the corridor after Ms. Scott, his chest feeling as if it would burst. Before entering the room, he paused, took a deep breath and tried to steady himself. He met Annie's gaze and willed her to smile. She didn't. Her expression was tight. He squeezed her hand, then turned and entered the room.

His breath hitched. Baby Elysha was in the arms of an older woman seated on a chair. Elysha was wrapped in a pink blanket and looked like an angel. Tears welled in his eyes. This was his daughter. His flesh and blood. He'd never let her out of his sight.

"Mr. Daley. Take a seat," Ms. Scott instructed.

He blinked. "Sorry. I couldn't take my eyes off her. She's beautiful."

"She is. This is Susan Hancock. She'll be doing the handover with you shortly."

He smiled at the woman in the chair. "Nice to meet you. This is Annie, my partner." He placed his hand lightly on the small of her back. Annie smiled and said hello.

"Nice to meet you both," Susan replied in a friendly voice. "We're going to be sorry to let this little miss go." She gazed down at Elysha and kissed the top of her head.

He sat and Annie sat beside him. He squeezed her hand.

Ms. Scott spread her hands on the desk. "There's some paperwork to sign, and then Susan will do the handover. You must be excited, and maybe a trifle nervous?"

He nodded. "Yes. Both. But we're ready for this. We can't wait to get her home."

"I hope you're ready for sleepless nights." She let out a small laugh and then turned her attention to the paperwork. He felt a little overwhelmed as she explained each form. Disclosures, disclaimers, warnings. He went ahead and signed them. "When can we have her name changed?"

"Any time you wish. She's your daughter, Mr. Daley."

He gulped. It was finally sinking in. When they walked out this door, this tiny bundle would be totally dependent on him and Annie. "That's great. We'll get it sorted."

"One last thing. Justice Bowman requested that you allow the mother's family access to Elysha. She would like you to sign this acknowledgment form."

He gritted his teeth but replied calmly, "Sure, that's fine. Where do I sign?"

She pointed to a line at the bottom of the form. "Here."

He signed it, but he was determined not to heed it.

"Here are their contact details. They'll also be given yours." She paused, removed her glasses, and then pinned him with her gaze. "You'd do well to befriend them, like Justice Bowman encouraged you to do."

He shrugged. "We'll see."

"Okay. That's the end of the paperwork. I'll hand you over to Susan now." She stood, shook their hands, and then left the room.

Susan smiled at them. "Have you had anything to do with babies before?"

"No, but we're eager to learn," Colin replied, squeezing Annie's hand and glancing at her, willing her to show some enthusiasm.

"You'd think caring for a baby would be simple. They're so tiny, but they can be very demanding and it's easy to become flustered. The foster mother has written down some notes for you. Elysha is still having feeds every three hours because she's so small. I suggest you take it in turns to attend to her at night. A nurse will visit twice a week at your home to begin with, but you'll also need to take her to the baby clinic once a week to be weighed and checked. If you have any concerns, we're only a phone call away." She went on to explain a number of things, and finally asked if they had any questions.

Colin shook his head. "No. I think we're good."

"As long as you're sure. Who's going to take her?" She looked first at Annie and then at Colin.

"I'll take her," he replied, pushing to his feet.

"Sit back down. I'll hand her to you."

He chuckled. "Sorry. You can tell I'm excited."

She laughed. "Yes. It's good to see." She stood and stepped towards him. When she placed Elysha into his arms and his daughter opened her eyes and looked at him, he couldn't stop the tears from streaming down his cheeks. "Hello, beautiful. I'm your daddy." Kissing the top of her head, he exhaled a long sigh of contentment.

WALKING PAST THE NURSERY, Natalie bid herself not to turn her head, but the pull was too strong. Her chest felt constricted. Tight. Heavy. She'd cried so many tears she doubted she had any left, but fresh tears found their way to her eyes when she stepped inside the room. The room where Elysha should have been sleeping. She picked up a baby blanket and pressed it against her face. It was so soft. She swallowed hard and eased herself onto the rocking chair. Elysha would be home with Colin Daley by now. Her heart clenched even more. Did he and his partner know what to do? Did they know how to feed her? How to change her nappy? To bathe her? To stop her crying? *Would she feel loved?*

Natalie closed her eyes and prayed. It was all she could do.

CHAPTER 21

olin couldn't wipe the grin off his face as he and Annie strolled along the street pushing Elysha in her pram. It was the best day of his life by far. Armed with formula, bottles, nappies and wipes, they had everything they needed, other than a cot. But she was so tiny, she could sleep in a drawer until they got one, although it might not go down too well with the nurse. He'd go back out and get one just as soon as they got home.

They managed the return bus trip without drama. Having a baby in the pram made such a difference. People stopped, offered help, cooed and aahed. They asked how old she was. What her name was. He answered each person readily. Annie just stood there and raised her brow at him. He shrugged and squeezed her hand. "Relax, Annie. It's all good." He was disappointed that she hadn't warmed to Elysha yet, but it would happen. How could anyone resist falling in love with this beautiful little girl?

Reaching the apartment block, Colin stopped and scratched his head. "We'll have to lift her out of the pram to carry her up. If I get her out, can you carry her while I carry the pram?"

Annie shrugged. "Guess I don't have a choice."

He pursed his lips, bent down and unfastened the buckle, and then slipped his hands beneath his little daughter. He lifted her out carefully and rocked her in his arms when she whimpered. "There, there. It's okay. Daddy's got you." He kissed her little cheek. Her skin was soft against his lips and she smelled of talcum powder and scented soap. He inhaled the scent slowly, taking it all in. Committed it to memory. It was such a special moment.

Beside him, Annie cleared her throat. "Are you going to give her to me anytime soon?"

"Yes. I was just enjoying holding her. I think she's settled. Hold your arms out."

Annie complied but looked awkward.

"Relax, Annie."

He settled Elysha in her arms. Elysha began to whimper again, but her cry was so tiny, he didn't know what there would be to complain about.

"What do I do?" Annie asked.

"Rock her gently. Talk to her."

"Talk to her? I'd rather put a pacifier in her mouth."

"We don't have one."

"You'd better get one."

"Okay. You go up. I'll fold the pram and follow you."

He gazed after Annie as she started up the stairs. He hoped that by the time they reached the apartment, she and Elysha would bond. Once out of sight, he turned his attention to the pram. Flustered, he tried all the levers, but eventually gave up and carried it up the stairs unfolded. He'd figure it out later.

He heard the cry before he reached the apartment. Leaving the pram in the stairwell, he sprinted the last flight of stairs and fled inside. "Annie, what's happened?"

"Nothing. She just won't stop crying."

He took Elysha and rocked her. "Shh, little one. It's okay. Daddy's got you." When she settled, he shifted his gaze to Annie. "You must have done something."

"Nope. She doesn't like me. It's obvious."

He tried not to let Annie's cool, aloof manner weigh him down. It was only a matter of time before she came around. Didn't all women have maternal instincts? "She'll warm to you. I know she will."

"I doubt it."

"Give her time. Maybe she's hungry. It might not be you at all."

"Well, you'd best feed her."

"I need help, Annie. I can't do this on my own. You know that."

She huffed. "What do you want me to do?"

"Make a bottle?"

She rolled her eyes. "I guess I can do that." She took out the can of baby formula and read the label. "Are the bottles clean?"

"They should be. We just bought them."

"I think they need washing."

"Okay. Do what you think. But hurry."

"It also says we have to use cooled boiled water. That's going to take time."

Colin groaned. "I don't think she can wait that long." He bounced Elysha when she began whimpering again.

"You decide. She's your baby."

Annie's words cut him to the quick. "She's *our* baby, Annie." Her brow lifted and they stared at each other like two bulls in a ring. She gave in first. "Fine. I'll boil some water and put it in the freezer."

"Good. I'll check her nappy while it's cooling."

"Don't ask me to do it."

"Don't worry, I won't." He was seething inside but tried not to show it. Setting his angst aside, he turned his attention to his daughter. "Okay, little one. I've never done this before, so be patient." She grew quiet, almost as if she understood. He placed her carefully on a blanket on the couch and then grabbed the bag of nappies and wipes. Slowly, he unclipped her jump suit and pulled the tabs on her nappy. He breathed a sigh of relief when it was only wet. He pulled a baby wipe from the packet and cleansed her tenderly. Her legs were thin but long. She seemed to be studying him, and his heart warmed. Taking a clean nappy, he positioned it underneath her and fastened it, then did up the clips on her jumpsuit. "There, that was painless." He smiled at her, lifted her up, and then kissed her, his heart overflowing with love. "How's the water going, Annie?"

"Still cooling," she called from the back room.

He groaned. She'd already returned to her painting. "Okay. I'll keep an eye on it." As he walked around the room rocking Elysha, trying to keep her quiet, he remembered the pram. About to ask Annie to hold Elysha while he retrieved it, he immediately thought better of it and instead laid Elysha on the couch. She wasn't going anywhere and he'd only be a minute.

As soon as he was out the door, she began crying. He turned and picked her up. Shushed her. When she was once again calm, he laid her down once more. The same thing happened. "Annie. Come and help. Please." Frustration sounded in his voice.

"What?" She stood in the doorway, hand on hip.

"Can you get the pram? It's halfway down the stairs."

She frowned. "What's it doing there?"

He shook his head. How had she not noticed that he'd raced up the stairs without it? "Don't worry. I'll get it." He shifted Elysha in his arm so he had one hand free and held her tight as he went downstairs. He sensed it was going to be like this, so he'd better get used to it.

By the time he scrambled up the stairs with the pram, Elysha was screaming. "Is that water ready yet?" he yelled. Annie appeared from the back room. "I'll check. Can't you keep her quiet? It's deafening."

"I'm trying." He shushed and he shushed, but nothing seemed to work. "Can't you hurry?"

"I am. Do it yourself if you can do better."

He didn't respond. If he put Elysha down, she'd scream even more and he couldn't prepare a bottle while holding her.

Finally, it was ready and Annie carried the bottle to him.

"Have you tested it?"

She looked at it him like he'd grown horns. "I'm not going to drink it."

"On your arm. Sprinkle some on your arm. Make sure it's not hot."

"How did you know to do that?"

"That woman told us. Weren't you listening?"

"No."

He shook his head. How was this going to work? "Pass the bottle to me."

She handed it over. He sat on the couch and sprinkled some milk onto his arm. It felt okay. "All right, little one, here we go." He placed the nipple into her mouth and held the bottle up like the woman had said. Elysha sucked hungrily. The silence was such a relief.

"Why are so you against her, Annie?" he asked later when Elysha had finished the bottle and was asleep on the couch.

She shrugged. "I've never liked babies, or kids, for that matter."

"But you've never been around them."

"Exactly."

"Can't you try? Look at her. Isn't she beautiful?" He put his arm around Annie when she sat beside him.

She shifted her gaze to Elysha. "I guess she's kind of cute. When she's asleep."

Hope built inside him. "I'll look after her until you feel you want to help. I'll manage somehow."

"What about work?"

He shrugged. "I'll take time off."

"So, you want me to earn the money?"

"You can't have it both ways, Annie."

She blew out a slow breath. "Okay. As long as you keep her quiet."

"I'll do my best."

. . .

IT WAS TOO late to go buy a cot by the time Colin remembered. The shops were already closed. Elysha would have to sleep in the pram. Annie prepared dinner and they watched a movie while they ate. She made up another bottle, gave it to him and then kissed him on the cheek. "I've got to go to work. Hope she's good for you."

He smiled. "She'll be fine. See you in the morning."

After she left, Colin let out a happy sigh as he stood and gazed at Elysha. She looked so peaceful asleep on the couch, wrapped in her little baby blanket. How could Annie not warm to her?

His peace lasted ten minutes. Elysha woke and began crying. He quickly grabbed the bottle, tested it, and then tried to put it between her lips, but she wouldn't take it. Then he remembered he had to burp her. He hadn't done that when he'd fed her before. He put her against his chest and patted her back. Finally, she let out a small burp. And another. And then he felt warm, gooey liquid running down his chest. He looked down. She'd been sick. He grabbed a cloth and wiped it while sniffing something horrid. He guessed it was her nappy, and he was right. He gagged as he cleaned her and fitted a fresh one.

"Maybe now you'll take your bottle." He tried again and breathed a sigh of relief when she took it. This time, when she finished, he remembered to burp her, and within fifteen minutes she was asleep on his chest. He set the bottle down and relaxed, enjoying the sensation of her little body rising and falling as she breathed in and out. He felt his eyelids flutter, and soon, he too was asleep.

CHAPTER 22

*T*wo days after the court awarded Elysha to Colin Daley, Natalie was listening to worship music while she sifted through her teaching materials. Having expected to be a full-time mother by now, she'd taken leave from work, but now that everything had changed, she wished she hadn't. A temporary teacher had been employed to look after her class for the term, and it was too late to reverse that.

Adam would be returning to work shortly now that the summer holidays were coming to an end. He'd also be studying for his Master's Degree, which meant he would be busy. Natalie had always worked. What was she going to do now? Staying at home would give her too much time to think about Elysha. She'd go stir crazy. She had to think of something to occupy her time.

She'd received numerous phone calls from friends and fellow teachers offering their condolences. No one could believe that the court hadn't given Elysha to them. They all asked what she was going to do. She said she didn't know. She drew a breath and released it slowly. "Lord, please give me direction. I'm at a loss."

Another half hour passed. All of her materials were sorted neatly in boxes and folders. But having no use for them, she carried them into the study. Adam was sitting at the desk working on his computer. She set the boxes down and placed her hand on his shoulder. "What are you doing?"

He rolled the chair back and pulled her onto his lap. "School work. Nothing terribly important. What are you doing?"

She shrugged. "I'm not sure." Her voice faltered.

He pulled her close and rubbed her back. "You'll work something out."

She sat for a few moments. "Do you think we can call Colin?"

"I doubt he'll answer, but we can try."

"I'd like to know Elysha's okay, even if we can't see her yet."

"I know, sweetheart. She's on your mind day and night."

"She is. I can't help it."

"I can understand that. Let me find his number."

She slipped off his lap and stood behind him while he sifted through his paperwork, finally lifting out the piece of paper the court had given them. He looked up. "Are you sure you're ready?"

She nodded. Her heart pounded as he dialed the number. It rang, but there was no answer, so Adam left a message. "Colin, this is Adam Jenkins. We're wondering how Elysha is doing. Can you please call me back? Thank you."

As Adam ended the call, Natalie was left with an inexplicable feeling of emptiness. "He's not going to call us, is he?"

Adam grimaced. "It's unlikely. I'll try again later."

"Okay. Would you like a cup of tea?"

"That would be nice. Thank you."

Natalie headed to the kitchen and turned the kettle on. "Heart of Worship", one of Natalie's favourite worship songs, was playing. She sang along quietly while she popped tea bags into the mugs and took out some homemade cookies and placed them onto a plate.

King of endless worth
No one could express how much You deserve
Though I'm weak and poor
All I have is Yours, every single breath
I'll bring You more than a song,
for a song in itself
Is not what You have required
You search much deeper within through the way things appear
You're looking into my heart
I'm coming back to the heart of worship
And it's all about You, all about You, Jesus
I'm sorry, Lord, for the thing I've made it
When it's all about You, all about You, Jesus

While she sang, her spirit lifted as the words reached deep inside her. Worship took her mind off herself and her problems and focused it instead on Jesus and gave her a sense of peace amidst her turmoil.

When she reached the study with the cookies and tea, she smiled at Adam. "I think I'd like to go out."

He looked up, surprised. "That's a great idea. Where would you like to go?"

"The beach?"

"Sounds good. Manly or Bondi?

"Bondi. We might see Simon."

"Okay. I'll finish this and be ready in ten."

"Great. I'll get ready, too." She snatched a cookie off the plate and carried it and her tea into the bedroom. She set the mug on the dresser and munched on the cookie while she changed into her swimsuit and packed towels and sunblock into a bag.

Adam appeared a few minutes later, and after quickly changing into his trunks, they were in the car heading to Bondi Beach.

It was a glorious summer day, and as they crossed the harbour bridge, Natalie gazed over the sparkling harbour and thought how blessed they were to live in such a beautiful place. She and Adam had everything they could possibly need or want, other than a child. She was hesitant to suggest they try another round of fertility treatment. The last two attempts had been unsuccessful and the whole process was uncomfortable. Their only other options were to foster or adopt. The adoption waiting list was years long. Fostering was the quickest option, but there was the risk that whatever child they were given might be taken from them after a time. Could she bear to hand a child back, and then do it all over again? People did it, but often after they'd had their own children. She and Adam would need to think and pray long and hard about that option. But for now, she'd simply enjoy a day at the beach. Enjoy the feel of sand between her toes. Salt spray on her face. The crash of waves as they reached the shore. The coolness of the water on her body. A time to refresh. To regroup.

They arrived at the beach half an hour later. She climbed out of the car and breathed in the salty air. Being a Saturday, the beach was crowded, but they managed to find a patch of sand not far from the water. Natalie set her bag down and slipped her sun dress off. Adam took his shirt off and asked her to rub sunblock onto his back. She squeezed some onto her hand and rubbed it in slowly. His olive skin was slightly tanned, but the Sydney sun could be ruthless, so protection was still needed. She didn't hurry. Instead of simply rubbing the sunblock on, she massaged it slowly into his back. His body was toned and trim, his shoulders broad and strong. Although not super muscly, he didn't carry an ounce of fat. And she loved him. Regardless of whether they had a child or not, she loved him. The realisation came softly and gently, like the breeze skimming her face. They'd placed so much emphasis on having a child that they'd been neglecting each other.

Her pulse skittered alarmingly as she realised she longed for him to hold her. To kiss her. She swallowed hard. They were on a beach amongst hundreds of others.

"Are you finished or are you daydreaming?" He turned his head, a grin on his face.

"I'm done. Can you do mine?"

"Sure."

She closed her eyes and enjoyed the touch of his hand on her skin. But it was over all too soon.

"Come on, I'll race you." He tossed the tube onto the towel and sprinted for the water.

She raced after him and fell into his arms as a wave

knocked her off her feet. They landed in the water, and as they surfaced, he held her tight and brushed sandy hair off her face. "Are you okay?"

"Yes. Perfectly okay. Kiss me."

His mouth covered hers hungrily and she felt the heady sensation of his wet, salty lips pressing against hers. Time stood still until another wave crashed over them. He held her firmly, and when the water subsided, they laughed.

Natalie didn't want the day to end. It had been so long since they'd been out on their own, with no purpose other than to enjoy each other's company and have fun.

"Let's have dinner out," Adam suggested as the sun began to disappear over the buildings, casting long shadows across the sand.

"Sounds wonderful, but we're not dressed to go out."

"We don't need to dress up for fish and chips."

She laughed. "I guess not. Fish and chips sounds great."

They headed to the strip of shops bordering the beach and wandered along until they reached *The Battered Cod*, the fish and chip shop they always ended up at when at Bondi. Adam placed their order while Natalie found an outside table. Bondi was one of those places that attracted tourists and locals alike. An eclectic mix, Natalie could people watch all day. They all had stories, histories, hurts, and needs. She often looked at people and wondered what their story was.

Catching sight of a familiar figure strolling towards them, she stood, raised her hand, and waved. "Simon!" He looked her way and when their gazes met, his face lit up. He was with another man she guessed was Ellis.

The two pushed their way through the crowd and stopped

at the side of the balustrade separating the eating area and the walkway. "What are you doing here, Nat? Is Adam with you?" Simon glanced around.

"He's inside ordering. We had a day at the beach. It was good to get out."

"I bet it was. It was a great day to be on the beach. Oh, this is my friend, Ellis." He turned and smiled at the man who sported a shadow of a beard and longish blond hair. A real surfer, but from what Simon had told them about him, his true passion was in helping others.

She smiled. "Nice to meet you. I'm Natalie, and Adam's around somewhere."

"Here I am." He placed his hand on her shoulder. "Hey, Simon, we were wondering if we'd see you down here."

"And you did. This is Ellis. Ellis, Adam, my brother-in-law." They shook hands over the balustrade.

"Why don't you join us?" Adam asked. "We can make room."

The two men exchanged glances. Ellis shrugged. "Sure." They strolled around and pulled up some chairs.

"I'll place the order," Ellis said before he sat. "Won't be long." He disappeared into the crowd.

Adam poured water for them all and Natalie took a sip of hers. "He looks like an interesting guy."

"He is. He's helped me a lot," Simon replied.

"How's Andy?"

Simon shrugged. "Not too good. I saw him last night. He was wasted."

"Oh, that's sad. I hope he sorts himself out soon." She flicked some hair over her shoulder. "Have you had your test done yet?"

"I'll do it next week."

"Putting it off?"

He grimaced. "Something like that."

Her heart went out to him. She squeezed his wrist. "It's not the end of the world if you have it."

"I know. It's just..." He shrugged. "If I have HIV, it'll remind me of my old life that I'm trying to leave behind."

"The Apostle Paul struggled with that. He had a thorn in the flesh, but he treated it as a gift. I know that sounds contradictory, but thorns and challenges, in whatever form they come, can draw us closer to God and build our character, if we let them." The words applied to her as well. Being childless was a thorn in the flesh. Realising she loved Adam with all her heart and soul, whether they had a child or not, was a huge revelation and was so freeing. Natalie thanked God silently for the insight.

He shrugged. "I've still got a lot to learn. I won't put it off."

"Good."

"Have you heard from Colin?" Simon asked.

Natalie let out a huge sigh. She wasn't upset with him for asking, but she'd been enjoying the day without constantly thinking about Elysha. "No. Adam tried calling him this morning but didn't get through."

"I can find him if you like."

"No. It's best to wait. We don't want to force anything."

"But Elysha should be with you."

"Maybe that's not what God had in mind for her." Natalie toyed with a strand of her salty hair.

"How could it not be?"

"We don't know His thoughts, Simon. Sometimes we

simply have to let go and trust Him. He is God, after all."

He sat back and folded his arms. "Like I said, I've got a lot to learn."

"We all do. Don't worry," Adam added as Ellis returned and sat down.

"What have I missed out on?" Ellis asked.

Natalie shrugged. "Just family catch up stuff."

"Simon told me about your niece. I'm so sorry," Ellis said quietly.

Natalie smiled appreciatively. "It's okay. We're dealing with it."

"That's good to hear. If ever you want a friendly ear, let me know. I'm a good listener."

"Thank you. We'll keep that in mind. I believe you've taken my little brother under your wing?"

Ellis grinned and winked at Simon. "You could say that. He's a cool dude."

"We're grateful you helped him that day. Thank you."

"You're welcome. I was just walking by. I think it was a God thing."

"You might be right."

Adam's order was called. "Excuse me, I'll be right back."

While he was gone, the three continued chatting. Ellis was easy to talk with. Natalie saw why he'd be a good counsellor—he didn't try to dominate the conversation and he listened more than he spoke.

Adam returned with his and Natalie's meals. "You're welcome to share."

"Thanks." Simon snatched a chip off the plate and stuffed it in his mouth.

"We should give thanks, Simon," Natalie said pointedly.

"Oh, right. Sorry." He closed his eyes and bowed his head.

Natalie tapped Adam's leg, and he, Natalie and Ellis closed their eyes while he gave thanks. "Lord, we thank You for Your abundant provision in our lives. You are a good God. Teach us to trust You in every aspect of our lives. We thank You now for this food. Bless it to our bodies. In Jesus' precious name. Amen."

A round of 'Amens' followed. Adam positioned the plates between the four of them and they shared the generous-sized meal together. There was plenty for them all. When Ellis's order was called, he went and collected it but returned with it wrapped in paper.

"You're not going to eat it?" Natalie asked.

"Not unless you want more. I'll find some homeless people to give it to."

She shook her head. "No, that was plenty for me. You're very kind."

He shrugged bashfully. "Not really. I was homeless once. I know what it's like."

Natalie angled her head. There was definitely a story there. "I'd like to hear about it one day."

He smiled. "Sure."

"Maybe I could write your story."

"Are you a writer?" He looked interested.

"No, but since I've got this term off, I thought I might try my hand at it."

Adam jerked his head around, his brow creasing. "When did you decide that?"

She chuckled. "Just now."

CHAPTER 23

*S*lumped on the couch, Colin replayed the voice message for the tenth time that day. It was short and undemanding, and the guy sounded calm. He didn't even ask to see Elysha—he simply asked how she was. That was just as well, because there was no way he could invite them here. The place was a mess. The nurse hadn't said as much that morning when she visited, but she wasn't impressed. Her nose was in the air most of the time. He clenched his fists. She was all of twenty. *What would she know about looking after a baby on your own?* He hadn't told her that. He'd simply said that Annie was at work. It wasn't a lie. She was in the back room, painting. Where she was now. He stared down the hallway. He was beyond being sad about her not bonding with baby Elysha. He was angry. The way she ignored Elysha made him seethe, and the silence between them was growing unbearable. She'd promised to help him, but he was realising her promise had meant nothing. She had no interest in raising Elysha.

His breaths came faster. He had to say something to her. He couldn't do this on his own. He loved Elysha, but she hardly stopped crying. It was driving him insane. Right on cue, she started again. He raked his hands through his hair. *What was wrong with her?* The nurse said it was normal for her to cry. But this much? He didn't think so. He pushed to his feet and walked to the cot he'd bought the day before and lifted her out. "There, there, Lysha. Shhh. Shhh." He rocked her and tried to calm her. Her little face was growing redder by the second, and her cries were escalating. "What's wrong with you? Why won't you stop crying?" He felt like crying himself. It was all too much. A heaviness grew in his chest as he prepared her bottle with one hand. Why wasn't Annie coming to help? Surely, she could hear Elysha screaming.

He placed the bottle in a jug of hot water to warm it while jigging Elysha in his other arm. Her cries persisted. The tension in his head increased. He thumped the counter. "Stop it! Just stop it!" Tears streamed down his cheeks. "I'm sorry, Elysha. I didn't mean it." He kissed her head. "I'm sorry. Forgive me." Taking the bottle from the jug, he quickly tested it and offered it her, but she didn't want it. "What's the matter? Shhh. Shhh." He offered it again. This time she began sucking and the room finally went quiet.

Colin eased himself onto the couch and his breaths began to slow. This wasn't how it was meant to be. Annie was supposed to be helping. Instead, Elysha was pulling them apart. But could he give her up? After he'd fought so hard for her? He gazed at her little face and swallowed the despair clogging in his throat. He'd so wanted to do this. But could he do it on his own? Without Annie?

Tears trickled down his cheeks. His dream was dying.

THREE DAYS LATER, his phone rang again while he was rocking Elysha in her pram trying to get her to sleep. Annie was at work, and his eyes had been drooping after yet another disturbed night. The shrill ring of the phone pulled him out of his drowsiness. Recognising the number as Adam's, he initially ignored it, but at the last second, he decided to answer it. He needed to talk to someone. Anyone. "Hello."

"Colin?" The guy sounded surprised he'd answered.

"Yes."

"It's Adam Jenkins. I'm calling to see how Elysha is doing."

Colin swallowed hard and looked at the tiny figure in the pram. "She's doing well."

"Do...do you think we could see her?"

He drew a slow breath as a war of emotions raged within him. He was so tired he could hardly think straight. "Yeah, yeah. We can meet somewhere." He scrubbed his face with his hand.

"Really? Where would you like to meet?"

He thought quickly. They couldn't come here. "The park. There's a park down the road. Dunstan's. We can meet there."

"Great. When?"

"This afternoon?"

"About three?"

"I'll see if I can make it. It depends on Elysha." He swallowed hard. What was he doing?

"We'll get there early. Get there when you can."

"Okay."

The call ended and Colin slumped against the back of the couch. He didn't think they would, but what if they caused trouble? Tried to take Elysha from him?

She whimpered and he began pushing the pram again. But maybe they could help stop her crying. It was worth the risk.

~

NATALIE'S EYES widened as she listened to Adam arranging the meeting. She hadn't expected Colin to answer his phone, let alone agree to a meeting. She couldn't stop herself squealing with anticipation.

When he ended the call, she flung her arms around him. "Praise God! We're going to see Elysha!" Joy bubbled inside her.

"Whoa, Nat! Calm down." But his eyes twinkled and she laughed at his grin, which was as large as a Cheshire cat's.

"This is wonderful, Adam. I can't wait to see her. We should take a gift. A new outfit. Nappies. Formula."

"I know you're excited, but I don't think we should overdo it. The guy sounded a little down."

She suddenly grew serious. "Did he mention Annie?"

"No."

She drew a long breath. "Do you think they're having problems?"

He shrugged. "I don't know. I guess we'll find out."

"If he tells us the truth."

"Yeah, there's that."

"I need to call Mum. Let her know." Natalie pulled her phone from her pocket.

"She'll be pleased."

"She will." Natalie speed-dialed her mother's number, and after she didn't answer, was preparing to leave a message when she picked up, sounding breathless.

"Natalie. Sorry, Bruce and I are out riding and I couldn't get my phone out of the pocket of these silly jeans."

"Mum! You're not wearing jeans?" Natalie chuckled. Her mother had said she'd never be seen dead or alive in a pair.

"Whoops. That was a slip of the tongue."

"So, it's true. You've got a pair on?"

"Yes."

Natalie laughed at the resignation in her mother's voice. "And you're out riding!"

"Yes. I'm actually enjoying it. I should have done it earlier."

"I'm so pleased, Mum. I think it's great. And I'm calling with more great news."

"Nat…don't tell me? Elysha?"

"Yes! We're seeing her this afternoon."

"That's wonderful, sweetheart. I'm so excited for you."

"I was starting to think it would never happen. I should have had more faith."

"You've got plenty, Natalie. Sometimes it's hard being patient."

"Thank you. And yes. It is."

"What time are you seeing her?"

"Three o'clock."

"I'll be praying for you."

"Thanks, Mum. I appreciate it. I'll let you know how it goes."

"Thank you, sweetheart. I'll be waiting!"

After ending the call, Natalie checked the time before returning her phone to her pocket. *Midday.* Three hours until they saw Elysha. She closed her eyes and took several deep breaths. *Thank You, Lord. I'm so grateful for this turn of events. I'm so sorry for doubting You. I know You have this under control and that You're working it out for Your glory. I know Elysha will never be our child, but I pray You'll bless her and her new parents. Help us to love them, for Elysha's sake. In Jesus' name. Amen.*

She turned when soft footsteps sounded behind her. Adam approached and slipped his arms around her waist. She placed her hands around his neck and smiled. "This is a good day."

"It is." He traced her hairline with his finger before wrapping her in his arms.

"I'd almost given up hope of seeing her again," Natalie said quietly as she gazed over his shoulder into the nursery across the hallway.

"I know. God's answering our prayers, we just have to trust Him."

She nodded. He was right. It was a lesson she had to learn over and over again.

Needing to fill the time before leaving for the park, Natalie decided to bake some cookies to give to Colin and Annie as a gift. While she baked, she hummed along to worship music and prayed for God to bless their meeting with Elysha, Colin and Annie. She was under no illusion about how emotionally challenging the meeting would be. To see and hold Elysha, but then have to hand her back and come home without her would be one of the hardest things she'd ever have to do.

So do not fear, for I am with you; do not be dismayed, for I am your God. I will strengthen you and help you; I will uphold you with my righteous right hand.

Tears sprang to her eyes. She knew that, but it was wonderful to be reminded. *Thank You, Lord. Thank You. I trust You to give us strength to do this. To show love to Colin and Annie and to not be bitter. Help us keep our eyes on You and not on ourselves. Lord, I know You'll supply all our needs according to the riches of Your glory in Christ Jesus. Thank You.*

At last it was time to leave. Natalie had packaged the cookies into a box wrapped in clear cellophane paper and placed a pretty red bow on top. They planned to stop at the shops and buy a box of nappies. Something practical as well as something nice. She hoped Colin and Annie wouldn't be offended.

Adam parked the car alongside Dunstan's Park. It was a sunny summer day, but the park looked dreary and dark. Natalie couldn't help but compare it with the lovely open parks in their area which offered amazing views of the harbour and beyond. They were spoiled. Blessed. She knew that. And she also knew she shouldn't judge, but it was difficult not to when the park was so depressing. A row of cheerless, dilapidated workers' cottages bordered the park on one side, and she wondered if Elysha lived in one of them. She hoped not.

Faint sounds of children shouting and laughing came from somewhere inside the park. Maybe it wasn't so terrible after all. She pushed her car door closed and grabbed Adam's hand. "Did he say where to meet?"

"No, but it's not a big park. I'm sure we'll find them."

She nodded. They were fifteen minutes early. "Let's take a walk."

He led the way along an uneven paved pathway that wove around garden beds that might once have been filled with colourful annuals and perennials but now overflowed with weeds. She was surprised that anything could grow in this gloom. Clinging to Adam's arm, she forced herself to stay positive. Soon, the gloom lightened and gave way to an open area. A man pushed a small child on a swing and several slightly older children were chasing each other around the playground. Adam and Natalie nodded at the man and walked on, completing the circuit several minutes later. They found a bench seat not far from their car, sat down and waited.

The minutes ticked by slowly. Each time a car stopped, Natalie looked up, but did Colin and Annie have a car? They might arrive on foot. Her heart beat in her throat and her hands grew clammy. Adam rubbed her back.

Finally, she caught sight of Colin and it was almost impossible to steady her erratic pulse. She took a deep breath to try to calm herself. Annie wasn't with him. They stood as he approached. His face was pale and dark circles hung under his eyes. Her heart suddenly softened. Was he caring for Elysha on his own? Where was Annie?

They walked towards him, stopping when they reached him. The two men shook hands. Unsure what to do, Natalie shook his hand as well but couldn't help herself from snatching a glance inside the pram at the same time. Tears pricked her eyes and her throat constricted. Wearing a soft pink onesie, Elysha's eyes were open and she looked adorable.

"May I?" Natalie asked, brushing her eyes with the back of her hand.

"Go ahead. She's just had a bottle. Take this in case she's sick." Colin reached into the bag hanging from the handle and handed her a soft cloth.

Natalie thanked him and then leaned over the pram. Joy welled in her heart as she carefully lifted Elysha from the pram and cradled her in her arms. "Hello, little Elysha. I've missed you so much." She smiled at the little girl she hadn't seen since before she'd gone to foster care. She sidled next to Adam so he could see her. She smiled at Elysha and then lifted her gaze and spoke to Colin. "She's put on weight."

"She has. She's almost five pounds."

"Is she feeding okay?"

"Mostly."

"And how are you doing?"

Colin's eyes flickered and she sensed she'd hit a nerve. "Fine. We're doing fine."

"That's good to hear. We brought you a few things. I hope you don't mind." She nodded to Adam who handed him a bag containing the nappies and the cookies. "Something for you and something for Elysha."

Colin looked surprised but took the bag and glanced inside. His eyes lit up. "Thank you. You shouldn't have."

"We wanted to," Natalie said. "Would you like to walk or sit?"

"Walk."

"Okay. Do you mind if I carry her?"

"That's fine. At least she's not crying."

Natalie frowned. "Has she been crying a lot?"

"All the time." While the frustration in his voice tore at Natalie's heart, the reason why Elysha would be crying so much concerned her more.

"That must be hard for you. Has the nurse suggested a reason?"

He shrugged. "She said it was normal."

Natalie blew out a slow breath as she gazed down at Elysha. Maybe Colin had no idea how much babies cried, but he certainly sounded frustrated. "She seems content at the moment."

"For once. You must have the touch."

Natalie gulped. It certainly seemed as if Elysha knew her. She was still so tiny, but she was alert and Natalie sensed a bond still existed between them. But she had to return her to Colin. She had to remember that.

They walked on in silence. Adam kept his hand on the small of her back and kept glancing over her shoulder at Elysha, occasionally talking to her and taking hold of a finger. It was the most bittersweet thing Natalie had ever experienced.

The time passed too quickly and before she was ready, it was time to hand the baby back. She fought tears as she kissed Elysha's cheek. "God bless you, Elysha. We love you." She passed her to Colin and bit her lip so hard she tasted blood.

Colin placed her carefully into the pram and then stood. His lips twisted and Natalie sensed he was holding something back. She glanced at Adam and nudged him gently. He took the hint. "Is everything okay, Colin?"

His eyes moistened. "Everything's fine." He fastened Elysha into the pram and strode off the way he'd come.

CHAPTER 24

*T*ears blinded Colin's vision. He shouldn't have come. He shouldn't have let them see Elysha. It made everything worse. If only Annie would hold Elysha like Natalie did, then it would all be okay. He'd have it out with her. Now. He was tired of the way she'd been treating him since Elysha had come to live with them. But she'd still be at work. It didn't matter. He couldn't return to the apartment without confronting her. He steered the pram across the road and headed to *Devilles*.

Entering the darkened bar, he didn't need to wait for his eyes to adjust. Instead, he strode ahead, knowing exactly where Annie would be. Stopping in front of the bar, he looked for her, but she wasn't there. Instead, another girl was behind the bar. She looked up. "Can I help you?"

"I'm looking for Annie."

"She quit this morning. I'm her replacement."

Colin frowned. "She quit? This morning?"

"That's what I said."

He began to panic. What was she planning? He thanked the girl and strode outside and began pushing the pram down the footpath. Elysha began crying, but he ignored her. He had to find Annie. Stop her from leaving, if that's what she was doing. Elysha's cries escalated, but he couldn't stop. He pushed on, ignoring the looks from passers-by. Finally reaching the apartment block, he parked the pram in the stairwell, unfastened Elysha and sprinted up the stairs with her in his arms. Her cries momentarily stopped. Bursting through the door, he called out and found Annie in the back room at her easel, earphones on, packed bags sitting on the floor beside her.

She lifted her gaze and removed her earphones. "I wondered when you'd be back."

He quickly closed the distance between them. "What are you doing, Annie? I went to the bar and the girl behind the counter told me you've quit."

"I have. I'm going home."

"Home? To Sweden?"

She nodded.

"But...but, what about us?" He looked down at Elysha. Thankfully, she'd stopped crying.

"I told you it was her or me."

"But you also said you'd try."

"I did. We don't like each other."

"Give it longer, Annie. I'm sure you'll learn to love her."

"I don't think so. She's yours, Colin, not mine. You can care for her. I'm sure you'll figure everything out."

"But I don't want to do it on my own."

She stood, packed her paints away, and faced him. "I did a painting for you."

He stepped closer and peered at it. It was Paige. He lifted his gaze. "Why?"

She shrugged. "You seemed to love her more than you love me. Or at least, you love her baby more."

"That's not fair, Annie." He seethed with anger. "I chose you over Paige."

"But you've chosen her baby over me."

He clenched his fist. He could easily hit her. But he wouldn't. "Get out. I don't want to see you ever again."

"Don't worry. I'm going." She gathered her bags and left.

When the door slammed, he collapsed onto the floor and wept. When Elysha whimpered, he held her tight. Cuddled and kissed her. His tears dampened her head and face. "What are we going to do, Elysha?" Feeling utterly miserable, he closed his eyes. Maybe Annie was right and he did love Paige more than he loved her. Everything would have been different if Paige had been here instead of Annie. She would have loved Elysha, just like her sister loved her. Seeing her hold Elysha so tenderly had tormented him. She and her husband could give Elysha so much more than he ever could. But he couldn't give her up.

Opening his eyes, he struggled to his feet. Casting a glance at the painting, he gulped. Paige really had been a special person. He'd been stupid to have chosen Annie over her. He picked up the painting and showed it to Elysha. "This is your mummy, sweetheart. She was a good person." Fresh tears stung his eyes. "Come on, let's get you changed and fed."

The night dragged on forever. Elysha wouldn't settle. Colin couldn't sleep. Finally, the endless night passed and dawn came. With Elysha in his arms, he picked up his phone and called Adam.

HAVING BEEN SLEEPING LIGHTLY, Natalie woke to Adam's phone vibrating. Reaching over him, she picked it up and answered groggily. "Hello."

Someone on the other end was sniffing.

"Hello. Who's this?"

Another sniff. "It's...it's Colin. His voice was barely a whisper.

"Colin!" She shook Adam until his eyes flickered. He sat quickly and looked at her, puzzled.

She mouthed that it was Colin and his eyes enlarged.

"What's the matter, Colin? Is something wrong with Elysha?"

"You...you can have her."

Caught off guard, she whispered, "What did you say?"

"You can have her. I can't do this anymore." He broke into sobs that wrenched her heart.

She was speechless, stunned. He was giving Elysha to them? "Colin. What's happened?"

"She's gone. Annie's gone."

Her heart broke for him. "We'll come over. What's your address?"

Through sobs, he gave it to them.

"We'll be there as soon as we can. Hang in there."

"I'll try."

Natalie hung up and stared at the phone. This had to be a dream. It couldn't be real. But when Adam slipped his arms around her, she knew it was. Elysha was coming home.

Anticipation filled her as they drove to Colin's apartment. They'd beaten most of the morning traffic and had a quick run across the city. While Adam drove, she prayed silently for Elysha and Colin's safety. He'd sounded unstable and they'd been tempted to call Child Services. In the end, they decided not to. He loved her and wouldn't do anything to harm her.

Reaching the apartment block, they ignored the graffiti and litter and the pram in the stairwell and sprinted up the stairs. Adam knocked on the door and moments later, Colin opened it. He looked dreadful, as if he hadn't slept for a year. He handed Elysha to Natalie and then fell in a heap.

"Colin! Are you okay?" She patted Elysha on the back while Adam bent down and helped Colin from the ground.

He mumbled something unintelligible. She thought she heard Paige's name, but wasn't sure.

Adam draped one of Colin's arms around his shoulder and helped him inside and eased him onto the couch. Several pillows and a blanket were on it and Natalie guessed he'd been trying to sleep there. As soon as his head was down, his eyes closed and he began to snore.

When Adam stood, Natalie caught his gaze. Her lip was trembling and she blew out a shaky breath. "I can't believe this, Adam. Is he really giving Elysha to us?"

"It seems that way."

"The poor guy. He tried so hard. He must feel devastated."

Adam stepped close to her and rubbed her arms. "It doesn't have to be the end for him. We can let him see her as often as he wants."

Tears found their way slowly down her cheeks. "You're a good man, Adam. I'm sure he'd like that."

"Showing him love is the least we can do."

"You're right. Let's leave him a note. Ask him to call us when he wakes up."

"Good idea."

Natalie dug a pen out of her purse, but she had no paper. When she spied a piece on the table, her mouth fell open. It was a painting of Paige. Such a wonderful likeness, it was instantly recognisable. She showed it to Adam. "I wonder who painted this?"

"I don't know, but it's very good. Strange it would be on the table."

"I think a few strange things went on here." Casting her gaze slowly around the room, for the first time Natalie noticed how untidy it was. "I don't think Annie helped at all."

"I think you're right. But she may have painted this. Look." He pointed to the initials on the bottom right. *AS*.

"Curious."

"Very."

"We should pray for him."

Adam nodded and smiled. "Good idea." He shifted closer to Colin and placed his hand lightly on the sleeping man's shoulder. "Lord, bless this man. He's been through so much. He's tried so hard to be a good father to Elysha and we know he loves her, but he's hurting and he's exhausted. Be with him now, and may he come to see in time that You're the best Father anyone could have. Bless him dear Lord, and we also thank You for this dear little girl who's come back to us. Help us to be good parents and to raise her in the knowledge and love of the Lord. In Jesus' precious name. Amen."

CHAPTER 25

*T*hree months later

Wendy finished the final decoration on Elysha's dedication cake, stepped back, and smiled at her handiwork. Natalie had asked her to make the cake, and Wendy had put every ounce of love she had into it. Not only for Elysha, but for Paige, whom she hoped was smiling down from above at the way things had turned out for her little girl.

Colin had signed the adoption papers the day after he returned Elysha to Natalie and Adam, and the court granted them temporary custody while the application processed. Now she was officially theirs. She was growing into such a beautiful baby despite her rough start in life. God had blessed them greatly. And Colin was doing well after Bruce offered him a job on the farm. Not that Colin knew anything about horses, but he was eager to learn, and Bruce was enjoying having someone to share his passion with. Colin had even stopped wearing black so much and sometimes wore blue jeans and a checked shirt, making Wendy smile.

He was coming to church with them today for Elysha's dedication service at their old church. She and Bruce had been praying for him every day. He was seeking truth and they often had interesting discussions, and they prayed that one day soon he'd open his heart to the Lord and realise that He was the Father he was truly seeking.

Bruce entered the kitchen and slipped his arms around her waist and nuzzled her neck. "That looks scrumptious, darlin'."

She laughed and turned around. "Bruce! It's Sunday morning and we need to get to church. There's no time for smooching."

He chuckled. "I know. I just wanted to hold you for a moment."

She smiled as she held his gaze. "This is such a special day, I don't want to be late."

"And we won't be." He popped a kiss on her lips. "What can I do to help?"

"Carry the cake to the car?"

"I can do that."

She placed it carefully into a container and handed it to him. "On the backseat will be fine. I just need to grab my purse."

"Okay, love. Is Colin ready?"

"I think so. Call out to him on the way out."

"I will."

As Bruce headed outside with the cake, Wendy quickly tidied the kitchen, grabbed her purse and then followed him out to the car. They'd been attending the local church and were slowly making friends, but today, the service was being held at their old church which Natalie and Adam still attended. The church where she and Greg had married, where their three children had been dedicated, where Greg's and Paige's funeral services had been held, and now, where baby Elysha was being dedicated. It was like going home. So many memories, mostly wonderful, although some less so, but life was like that. There was a time for everything, and today was baby Elysha's special day. Wendy couldn't wait to see her in the pretty outfit Natalie had made for the occasion. Since she wasn't working, Natalie had time for sewing and cooking, and she'd even started writing that book she'd talked about. She hadn't told anyone what it was about, but she said they might be surprised. Wendy guessed it might be Paige's story, but she didn't know.

Bruce had just placed the cake onto the seat when Wendy arrived. Colin leaned against the car with one hand on the roof, chatting to Bruce about something or other. She had to smile. Bruce was so patient with him, listening to him talk about so many things. But then Bruce always came up with something Colin hadn't thought about which made him think.

He stopped talking and opened the front door of the car for her.

Wendy smiled. "No, it's okay. I'll sit in the back with the cake."

Bruce quirked a brow.

She caught his gaze and rubbed his back. "It's fine, darling. You and Colin can continue your chat."

He rolled his eyes but she knew he'd grown fond of Colin and enjoyed their conversations.

The trip took almost an hour. Wendy sometimes wished

they still lived on the harbour, but she and Bruce were making their own memories on their farm, and she knew that moving had been the right thing to. Plus, she never would have learned to ride a horse if they hadn't, nor bought a pair of jeans which she'd no doubt need when they visited Bruce's ranch back in Texas sometime soon.

Arriving at the church, Bruce parked the car beside Natalie and Adam's. He climbed out and opened the door for her while Colin opened the other door and lifted the cake out. Bruce placed his arm lightly around Wendy's waist and walked beside her along the path as they headed for the chapel. He knew how many memories this place held for her, and as always, he was her rock.

Colin walked behind them with the cake. When they reached the entrance to the chapel, Wendy turned and said she'd take it and put it in the hall kitchen. "I won't be long. Go in if you like."

They were early, but a number of parishioners had gathered at the entrance to the chapel and were chatting. Wendy sent up a quick prayer for Colin. This was going to be challenging for him. Not only being in church for the first time, but although he was Elysha's biological father, it would be Natalie and Adam carrying Elysha to the front, seeking God's blessing on her life, and committing to raise her in the ways of the Lord. It would be a surreal experience for him, but they'd talked about it at length and he'd accepted the situation. He was grateful that Natalie and Adam had invited him into their lives and allowed him to see Elysha whenever he wanted.

She hurried into the adjoining hall and smiled. Natalie was

jigging Elysha in her arms while chatting with her good friend, Ruth. She placed the cake container on the kitchen counter alongside other containers of baked goodies they were serving for morning fellowship after the service, and then joined Natalie and her friend. She kissed Natalie's cheek, smiled at Ruth, and held Elysha's hand. "And how's our little princess today?"

Natalie laughed. "Acting like one!"

"You wouldn't be misbehaving on your special day, would you?" Wendy winked at the baby. "May I take her?"

"Sure. She's all yours." Natalie passed her over, straightening the ends of the full-length dress.

"The dress is beautiful, Nat. You did a great job. And I love the little headband." Wendy fingered the headband that matched the ivory satin gown with organza skirt and bow.

"Thank you." Natalie smiled. "Well, I guess we should go in and find Adam."

"Yes, and Simon should be here by now." Wendy squeezed Elysha's little hand as she tried to grab her pearls. "No, you don't, missy." Wendy laughed, her heart warming.

They left the hall and entered the chapel. Bruce, Simon and Colin stood towards the front in the aisle. Adam was chatting with his parents and other members of his family who'd come to witness the dedication. Other worshippers had begun filing in and the chapel was starting to fill. Wendy waved at several of her friends. She'd catch up with them later, but her eyes lit up when her best friend, Robyn, entered and walked towards them. Robyn's elderly mother was still ill and she'd been caring for her almost around the clock with little respite, but she'd promised to be here for Elysha's dedication service. Wendy smiled and kissed her cheek. "It's so good to see you, Rob. Thanks for coming."

"I wouldn't have missed it for the world. And look at this little princess! She's gorgeous."

Wendy's heart expanded. Elysha was indeed gorgeous— God had blessed them greatly.

The worship band began playing. "We'd best sit," Wendy said. She handed Elysha back to Natalie and sat between Bruce and Robyn, while Natalie, Adam and Simon sat in the front row. Colin sat on the other side of Bruce. Her family. She was so blessed, and she knew that Greg and Paige were here in spirit. Bruce took her hand as they stood to sing one of her favourite new worship songs, "Everlasting God".

Strength will rise as we wait upon the Lord
We will wait upon the Lord, we will wait upon the Lord
You're the defender of the weak
You comfort those in need
You lift us up on the wings
Like eagles
From everlasting to everlasting
God, You are everlasting

Pastor Will McDonald was leading the service, and when he invited Natalie and Adam to the front a little later to dedicate Elysha to the Lord, Wendy struggled to contain her tears. Natalie had shared with her not long before Elysha was returned to them that she'd become content with the idea of being childless. But God had worked this out so there were no losers. It was more than she could have ever imagined or hoped for. But their God was an awesome God, reigning with wisdom, power, and love, so she shouldn't have been surprised.

Smiling, Pastor Will nodded to them as they reached the front. "A very warm welcome to Adam, Natalie and Elysha Jenkins and their families. Adam and Natalie have had quite a journey to get to this point, but today they've come to dedicate their daughter, Elysha Grace, to the Lord, and to promise, in front of this congregation and before God, to raise her according to God's Word.

"In this church, we don't baptise infants. We believe that Scripture teaches baptism as a personal choice for the believer. Clearly, an infant can't make the decision to be baptised or not to be baptised, so, we follow a centuries old tradition and heritage of presenting our children to God by way of dedication. We see this happening in the gospels when Christ's mother and father brought Him to the temple and presented him to God. In this day and age, we celebrate with a public confession and commitment on the part of the parents to raise their children according to God's Word, to teach them to obey His commands, and to do everything they can to bring them to a saving knowledge of Jesus Christ.

"Children are precious to God, and I'd like to read Mark chapter 11, verses 13 to 16. *'People were bringing little children to Jesus for Him to place His hands on them, but the disciples rebuked them. When Jesus saw this, He was indignant. He said to them, "Let the little children come to me, and do not hinder them, for the kingdom of God belongs to such as these. Truly I tell you, anyone who will not receive the kingdom of God like a little child will never enter it." And He took the children in His arms, placed His hands on them and blessed them."*

"Adam and Natalie, I believe you wish to say a few words?"

Adam nodded, smiled and stepped to the microphone. Natalie stood beside him, holding Elysha. He took a breath and gazed around the congregation. "Hello." He paused and took another deep breath. Natalie rubbed his back. They shared a smile and then he began, his voice, quiet but sincere. "Natalie and I thank God every day for Elysha Grace, who came to us via a circuitous route. Firstly, following the passing of Natalie's younger sister, Paige, who died giving birth to her, and then again by a generous and self-sacrificing act by her father, Colin, who allowed us to officially adopt her. We feel very blessed to be her parents.

"Elysha, we want you to know how very much you're loved and wanted. The scripture we want to encourage you with is Proverbs 3, verses 3 to 8. He placed his hand lightly on her head.

"*Let love and faithfulness never leave you; bind them around your neck, write them on the tablet of your heart. Then you will win favor and a good name in the sight of God and man. Trust in the Lord with all your heart and lean not on your own understanding; in all your ways submit to Him, and He will make your paths straight. Do not be wise in your own eyes; fear the Lord and shun evil.*'

"Elysha, we love you with all our heart, and with God's help, we promise to be the best parents we possibly can be. God bless you, sweetheart." He smiled at her, kissed her forehead, then moved to the side.

Pastor Will returned to the microphone. "Thank you for that, Adam. That was wonderful. I'd now like to ask you both the following question. Do you, Adam and Natalie, vow to provide an atmosphere and spiritual nurturing in your home that will incline Elysha's heart towards the gospel and a saving relationship with Jesus Christ?"

"We do."

He turned to the congregation. "Church family, will you please stand?" He paused a moment while everyone stood. "As brothers and sisters in Christ, do you agree to support and encourage the Jenkins' family as you teach and work with them in Sunday School and discipleship classes, in spontaneous conversations and in general fellowship, in the spiritual development of their daughter, Elysha?"

A united "We do" resounded strongly from the standing congregation.

"Thank you. Will all the family members come to the front before I pray?"

Wendy squeezed Bruce's hand. They'd debated whether Colin should be included, and now she felt strongly that he should. Bruce looked at her and unspoken words passed between them. He gave a short nod, turned to Colin and whispered in his ear. Colin's eyes widened. Bruce motioned for him to follow, which he did. Wendy grabbed his arm and walked with him to the front. She stood with her arms around both Colin and Simon, while Bruce stood behind them, his hands on her shoulders. Adam's family also joined the group at the front.

"What a lovely family. I know you've been through many challenges, but God is good, and I know you're there for each other, and that you'll give Adam and Natalie all the support they need to help raise Elysha. Now comes the best part of the morning! May I please take this precious little girl?"

Smiling, Natalie nodded and passed Elysha to Pastor Will.

He took her in his arms and smiled down at her. "She certainly is a beautiful little girl." Raising his head, he spoke to the congregation. "Let's pray."

The congregation bowed their heads and silence filled the chapel. Wendy stilled her heart before the Lord.

"Our God and Heavenly Father, what a precious moment this is. To bring this beautiful little girl before You and ask You to bless her is such a privilege. We pray that Elysha will be rooted and established in love, and that she may, together with all the Lord's holy people, grasp how wide and long and high and deep is the love of Christ, and to know this love that surpasses knowledge—that she may be filled to the measure of all the fullness of God.

"And I also ask you to bless her parents, Adam and Natalie. Give them guidance and wisdom as she grows. And Lord, I also ask a special blessing on her biological father, Colin. He loved her so much that he was prepared to give her up. Bless him, Lord, for that selfless act of love. And last of all, I pray for the extended family. Thank You for their strong faith. Help them to be a wonderful support system for Adam and Natalie, and for little Elysha as she grows.

"Elysha, The Lord bless you and keep you, The Lord make His face shine upon you, and be gracious to you; The Lord lift up His countenance upon you, and give you peace. And all the people said, 'Amen.'"

Wendy's heart overflowed with joy. Tears streamed down her cheeks. She couldn't help it. She was so blessed. God had been faithful and seen them through so many challenges. There would be more ahead, of that she was certain, but for now, she would enjoy the fellowship of her wonderful family and friends and thank God for His amazing grace and love. Bruce's firm, solid hand on her shoulder gave her strength. He passed her a tissue as they returned to their seat to sing the final hymn, one of her all-time favourites. She stood and sang it with gusto with her arm around Bruce's waist.

Crown Him with many crowns,
The Lamb upon His throne;
Hark! how the heav'nly anthem drowns
All music but its own!
Awake, my soul, and sing
Of Him who died for thee,
And hail Him as thy matchless King
Through all eternity.

LATER, while fellowshipping in the hall, Simon told her he'd taken the test. He was clear of HIV. She threw her arms around him and cried. He also told her he was starting an internship at The Emmaus Chapel—he was going to be a counsellor, like Ellis. She couldn't have been happier for him. "That's wonderful, Simon. I'm thrilled!"

It was hard leaving everyone, but later, when Bruce suggested they go for a late afternoon ride, Wendy readily agreed. She'd come to love the time they shared chatting and simply enjoying each other's company while exploring the quiet trails on horseback. They often stopped and chatted with their neighbours, and sometimes they stopped for a leisurely picnic at one of the many parks in the area. Life went on. She still grieved over Paige, but with God's help and Bruce's support, she'd learned to live with her grief, and having baby Elysha in their lives was the best blessing ever. The thought of leaving her to visit Bruce's family in Texas tore at her heart, but he needed to see them. It was time, and she knew that. And besides, they'd be coming back. This was their home.

NOTE FROM THE AUTHOR

I hope you enjoyed "A Time to Abide". I know it touched on some difficult and off-times contentious issues, but I pray that if nothing else, it will have made you think about God's amazing love for *all* mankind. "For all have sinned and fallen short of God's glory", "But God demonstrates His own love for us in this, while we were still sinners, Christ died for us." My prayer is that you and your loved ones will know the freedom and hope that new life in Jesus brings.

Wendy and Bruce's story continues in "A Time to Rejoice", which is available to pre-order now and will be available to read on KU on May 7.

To make sure you don't miss it, and to be notified of all my new releases, why not join my Readers' list. You'll also receive a free thank-you copy of "Hank and Sarah - A Love Story", a clean love story with God at the center.

Enjoyed "A Time to Abide"? You can make a big difference. Help other people find this book by writing a review and telling them why you liked it. Honest reviews of my books help bring them to the attention of other readers just like yourself, and I'd be very grateful if you could spare just five minutes to leave a review (it can be as short as you like) on the book's Amazon page.

Oh, and keep reading for a bonus chapter of "Tender Love". If you enjoyed "A Time to Abide", I'm sure you'll enjoy this one too.

Blessings,
Juliette

TENDER LOVE
Chapter 1
Brisbane, Australia

Early morning sunshine streamed through the white lace curtains of Tessa Scott's pocket-sized bedroom, but inside her heart, it rained. Nearly three months had passed since she had formally ended her relationship with Michael Urbane, and although she firmly believed it had been the right thing to do, pain still squeezed her heart whenever she thought of him.

Some days were easier than others, but the past two days had been especially hard. Yesterday had been Michael's birthday. How tempted she'd been to call him and at least wish him 'happy birthday'. Last year she'd surprised him with a day trip snorkelling on Moreton Island. They'd had so much fun—they always did, and the very memory of that wonderfully happy, sun-filled day only made it worse. She shouldn't let her mind go there, but she couldn't help it, and images of their day snorkelling amongst the coral and the myriads of brightly coloured fish played over and over in her mind.

Burying her head in her pillow, Tessa sobbed silent tears. It hurt so badly. If only the accident at his work hadn't happened. *Or he hadn't lied about the drugs.* She inhaled deeply as a sob escaped, sending another wave of sadness through her body. *Why couldn't she let go?* Maybe she should give him another chance? *But it would never be the same.* She knew that. Their adventure had died, and she needed to accept it.

A soft knock on the door interrupted her thoughts. The gentle but firm voice of her housemate, Stephanie, sounded on the other side. "Tess, you need to get up."

Tessa buried her head deeper in the pillows.

The door creaked open and Stephanie tip-toed in, placing a cup of spiced chai tea on Tessa's nightstand. The aromatic mixture of cardamom, cinnamon, ginger and other herbs filled the room, tickling her nose. Steph knew the trick to getting her up.

She gave in and raised her head. "What time is it?"

"Time to get up, that's what." Dressed in a smart business suit, Stephanie placed her hands on her hips and studied Tessa with an air of disapproval. "Don't tell me you've been crying over Michael again?"

Tessa sat up and took a sip of tea before meeting her friend's gaze. "Just thinking about him, that's all."

Stephanie shook her head and let out a frustrated sigh. "I know you're grieving, but it's been months since you broke up. Come on. Get out of bed and get ready for work. Your boss called and said she'd place you on unpaid leave if you call in sick one more time. I was tempted to tell her you weren't even sick."

"But I have been sick." Tessa leaned back against her bedhead and bit her lip, forcing herself not to cry in front of Stephanie.

"I know." Sitting on the edge of the bed, Stephanie took hold of Tessa's free hand. "It's hard to let go, especially having been together for so long. But breaking up was the only option. You know that."

"But maybe I was too hard on him." Tessa grabbed a tissue and wiped her eyes. "Those drugs changed him, Steph. He wasn't himself."

"I know. But you did try to help him. For months. I watched you slowly being torn apart. The truth is, you can't help someone who doesn't want to be helped." Stephanie squeezed her hand. "You can't help someone who lies to you about their addiction, even if it is to prescription drugs. *And he stole from you.* You need honesty in your relationship, and Michael wasn't willing to give that to you. You did the right thing. You're better off without him."

"It's just hard not knowing where he is or how he's doing." Tessa glanced at the photo of him still sitting on her dresser. "It's hard being single again. I feel …" She paused and searched for the right word, as the ache in her chest grew. "Lonely."

"You poor thing." Stephanie leaned forward and hugged her tightly. "I'm here for you, Tess. And so's God, you know that. I understand you feel bad about this whole situation, but God's with you, and He'll help you through it. And you never know what, or who, He might have in store for you!" She gently brushed the stray hair from Tessa's face and gave her another hug.

Tessa nodded reluctantly. Steph was right. She'd made the right decision and knew that God would be with her and would help her through it, but translating that knowledge to her heart was another matter altogether.

"Come on kiddo, breakfast's ready. Let's get you up, dressed, and off to work."

Tessa slid out of bed as Stephanie retreated to the kitchen. As she swallowed down the rest of her tea, Michael's photo caught her attention once again. Grey eyes with a hint of blue in a tanned, chiselled face stared out at her, tugging at her heart-strings. She picked up the photo and flopped back onto her bed, gazing at the face that was so familiar. This torture had to end. She traced the outline of his face with her finger before hugging the photo to her chest. Closing her eyes, she squeezed back hot tears. This was it. The end.

"*God, please help me get through this day.*" Her body shuddered as she gulped down unbidden sobs. "*I'm sorry it's taken so long, but I'm ready to let go. Please help me.*" Tears streamed down her face as she hugged the photo tightly one last time before she opened the bottom drawer of her dresser and stuffed the photo under the pile of chunky knit sweaters she rarely wore.

Time to move on, and with God's help, she would.

Grab your copy today to continue the story!

A grieving billionaire, a solo mother, and a woman determined to sabotage their relationship...

Her Disgraced Billionaire

A messed up billionaire who lands in jail, a nurse who throws a challenge he can't refuse...

"The Billionaires with Heart Christian Romance Series" is a series of stand-alone books that are both God honoring and entertaining. Get your copy now,

enjoy and be blessed!

The True Love Series

Set in Australia, what starts out as simple love story grows into a family saga, including a dad battling bouts of depression and guilt, an ex-wife with issues of her own, and a young step-mum trying to mother a teenager who's confused and hurting. Through it all, a love story is woven. A love story between a caring God and His precious children as He gently draws them to Himself and walks with them through the trials and joys of life.

"A beautiful Christian story. I enjoyed all of the books in this series. They all brought out Christian concepts of faith in action."

"Wonderful set of books. Weaving the books from story to story. Family living, God, & learning to trust Him with all their hearts."

The Precious Love Series

The Precious Love Series continues the story of Ben, Tessa and Jayden from the The True Love Series, although each book can be read on its own. All of the books in this series will warm your heart and draw you closer to the God who loves and cherishes you without condition.

"I loved all the books by Juliette, but those about Jaydon and Angie's stories are my favorites...can't wait for the next one..."

"Juliette Duncan has earned my highest respect as a Christian romance writer. She continues to write such touching stories about real life and the tragedies, turmoils, and joys that happen while we are living. The words that she uses to write about her characters relationships with God can only come from someone that has had a very close & special with her Lord and Savior herself. I have read all of her books and if you are a reader of Christian fiction books I would highly recommend her books." Vicki

∾

The Shadows Series

An inspirational romance, a story of passion and love, and of God's inexplicable desire to free people from pasts that haunt them so they can live a life full of His peace, love and forgiveness, regardless of the circumstances.

Book 1, *"Lingering Shadows"* is set in England, and follows the story of Lizzy, a headstrong, impulsive young lady from a privileged background, and Daniel, a roguish Irishman who sweeps her off her feet. But can Lizzy leave the shadows of her past behind and give Daniel the love he deserves, and will Daniel find freedom and release in God?

Hank and Sarah - A Love Story, *the Prequel to "The Madeleine Richards Series" is a FREE thank you gift for joining my mailing list. You'll also be the first to hear about my next books and get exclusive sneak previews. Get your free copy at www.julietteduncan.com/subscribe*

The Madeleine Richards Series

Although the 3 book series is intended mainly for pre-teen/ Middle Grade girls, it's been read and enjoyed by people of all ages.

"Juliette has a fabulous way of bringing her characters to life. Maddy is at typical teenager with authentic views and actions that truly make it feel like you are feeling her pain and angst. You want to enter into her situation and make everything better. Mom and soon to be dad respond to her with love and gentle persuasion while maintaining their faith and trust in Jesus, whom they know, will give them wisdom as they continue on their lives journey. Appropriate for teenage readers but any age can enjoy." Amazon Reader

The Potter's House Books...stories of hope, redemption, and second chances. Find out more here:

http://pottershousebooks.com/our-books/

The Homecoming

Kayla McCormack is a famous pop-star, but her life is a mess. Dane Carmichael has a disability, but he has a heart for God. He had a crush on her at school, but she doesn't remember him. His simple faith and life fascinate her, But can she surrender her life of fame and fortune to find true love?

Unchained

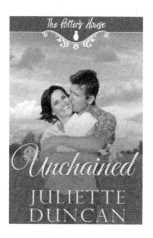

Imprisoned by greed – redeemed by love

Sally Richardson has it all. A devout, hard-working, well-respected husband, two great kids, a beautiful home, wonderful friends. Her life is perfect. Until it isn't.

When Brad Richardson, accountant, business owner, and respected church member, is sentenced to five years in jail, Sally is shell-shocked. How had she not known about her husband's fraudulent activity? And how, as an upstanding member of their tight-knit community, did he ever think he'd get away with it? He's defrauded clients, friends, and fellow church members. She doubts she can ever trust him again.

Locked up with murderers and armed robbers, Brad knows that the only way to survive his incarceration is to seek God with all his heart - something he should have done years ago. But how does he convince his family that his remorse is genuine? Will they ever forgive him?

He's failed them. But most of all, he's failed God. His poor decisions have ruined this once perfect family.

They've lost everything they once held dear. Will they lose each other as well?

Blessings of Love

She's going on mission to help others. He's going to win her heart.

Skye Matthews, bright, bubbly and a committed social work major, is the pastor's daughter. She's in love with Scott Anderson, the most eligible bachelor, not just at church, but in the entire town.

Scott lavishes her with flowers and jewellery and treats her like a lady, and Skye has no doubt that life with him would be amazing. And yet, sometimes, she can't help but feel he isn't committed enough. Not to her, but to God.

She knows how important Scott's work is to him, but she has a niggling feeling that he isn't prioritising his faith, and that concerns her. If only he'd join her on the mission trip to Burkina Faso...

Scott Anderson, a smart, handsome civil engineering graduate, has just received the promotion he's been working for for months. At age twenty-four, he's the youngest employee to ever hold a position of this calibre, and he's pumped.

Scott has been dating Skye long enough to know that she's 'the one', but just when he's about to propose, she asks him to go on mission with her. His plans of marrying her are thrown to the wind.

Can he jeopardise his career to go somewhere he's never heard of, to work amongst people he'd normally ignore?

If it's the only way to get a ring on Skye's finger, he might just risk it...

And can Skye's faith last the distance when she's confronted with a truth she never expected?

Billionaires with Heart Christian Romance Series

Her Kind-Hearted Billionaire

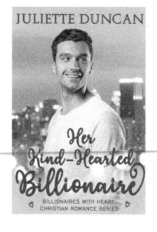

A reluctant billionaire, a grieving young woman, and the trip that changes their lives forever...

Since inheriting his grandfather's fortune and mining business with his two siblings, Nicholas Barrington has tried to make his grandfather proud, but he's tired of his siblings' selfishness and arrogance. When he stops by his local church on his way home one night, he hears about an organization in Bangkok that intrigues him, and he decides to take a month off work to volunteer.

Three weeks before her wedding, Phoebe Halliday receives the news no one ever wants to hear... her fiancé, Reed Fisher, has been killed in a car accident. Ten months later, she's still grieving and plagued by memories, so when her best friend suggests she takes time off work to accompany her on a three-month trip to South-East Asia, Phoebe jumps at it.

But the trip Holly has in mind is more than just a holiday. Her passion for helping others takes them to a mission in Bangkok where young girls and boys caught up in sex-trafficking are rescued and rehabilitated.

When Nick and Phoebe meet, she has no idea who Nick is, and she fights her growing affection for him as she feels she's being disloyal to Reed's memory.

Nick soon realizes that even though he's drawn to Phoebe, unless he shares her faith, they have no future other than friendship. But he won't make a fake commitment - not even to snag the girl of his dreams.

Can Phoebe let go of Reed and open her heart to new love, and can Nicholas open his heart to God and find not only new life, but a love he never dreamed existed?

~

Stand Alone Christian Romantic Suspense

Leave Before He Kills You

When his face grew angry, I knew he could murder...

That face drove me and my three young daughters to flee across Australia.

I doubted he'd ever touch the girls, but if I wanted to live and see them grow, I had to do something.

The plan my friend had proposed was daring and bold, but it also gave me hope.

My heart thumped. What if he followed?

Radical, honest and real, this Christian romantic suspense is one woman's journey to freedom you won't put down...get your copy and read it now.

ABOUT THE AUTHOR

Juliette Duncan is a Christian fiction author, passionate about writing stories that will touch her readers' hearts and make a difference in their lives. Although a trained school teacher, Juliette spent many years working alongside her husband in their own business, but is now relishing the opportunity to follow her passion for writing stories she herself would love to read. Based in Brisbane, Australia, Juliette and her husband have five adult children, seven grandchildren, and an elderly long haired dachshund. Apart from writing, Juliette loves exploring the great world we live in, and has travelled extensively, both within Australia and overseas. She also enjoys social dancing and eating out.

Connect with Juliette:

Email: juliette@julietteduncan.com

Website: www.julietteduncan.com

Facebook: www.facebook.com/JulietteDuncanAuthor

Twitter: https://twitter.com/Juliette_Duncan

Made in the USA
Monee, IL
04 November 2021

81112453R00118